Rest, Relax, Run for Your Life

Written By: Katherine Brown

Cover Design by: Breezy Reads

Copyright © 2019 by Katherine Brown
Visit Katherine at
www.katherinebrownbooks.com
All rights reserved.
ISBN: 978-1-7337258-1-1
Imprint: Katherine Brown Books

No part of this book may be reproduced in any form or by any electronic or mechanical means including information storage and retrieval systems, without written permission from the author, except for the use of brief quotations in a book review.

This is a work of fiction. Names, characters, businesses, places, events, locales, and incidents are either the products of the author's imagination or used in a fictitious manner. Any resemblance to actual persons, living or dead, or actual events is purely coincidental.

Table of Contents

Acknowledgements---------------5
Chapter 1-------------------------7
Chapter 2-------------------------27
Chapter 3-------------------------40
Chapter 4-------------------------48
Chapter 5-------------------------63
Chapter 6-------------------------73
Chapter 7-------------------------86
Chapter 8-------------------------101
Chapter 9-------------------------116
Chapter 10------------------------130
Chapter 11------------------------145
Chapter 12------------------------160
Chapter 13------------------------174
Chapter 14------------------------186
Chapter 15------------------------194
Chapter 16------------------------200
Chapter 17------------------------206
Chapter 18------------------------218
Chapter 19------------------------233
Chapter 20------------------------243
Chapter 21------------------------257
Human Trafficking Info----------267
Author Note----------------------273
Book 2 Sneak Preview------------274

Acknowledgments

Writing a book is a long process!

I want to thank Patrick and Lexi for all that you did at home to give me time to write this story and for loving me through all of my moods.

I want to thank each one of my incredible beta readers. Without you this book would have suffered from typos, long sentences, and Gladys wouldn't have found her new hobby. Thank you from the bottom of my heart: Cammie, Ginger, Kathy, Leslie, and Elicia.

Thank you to my fabulous cover designer at Breezy Reads. You went beyond my expectations.

This book would not have been possible without each one of you.

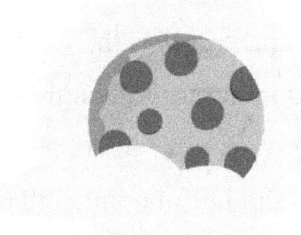

ONE

"Sam. Hey Sam!" I called out. "Sam, why is the news crew outside?"

My business partner and best friend, Samantha Lowe, poked her head out of the supply closet. She had been tucked away in that closet doing inventory since we arrived an hour ago. "What?" she asked. With her light brown hair pulled up in a sleek ponytail, the bottom half which she recently dyed a vibrant red, was very visible today, making me smile.

Samantha Lowe's only rebellious streak against her snobby, picture-perfect parents was the rainbow of colors she continuously displayed in her hair, changing it every few months, ever since she went away to college four years ago. Her parents were constantly disappointed that she showed no signs of outgrowing that phase.

Thanks to an impromptu girls' day at the hair salon yesterday, I am also sporting a more colorful look today; much more colorful than usual for me, at least.

Me? I'm Piper. I'm messy buns, cargo pants, and chocolate chip cookies for breakfast. I wouldn't call myself a tomboy, but I've never been a high heel and makeup kind of girl either.

My own dark brown, shoulder-length, wavy locks were typically drab in comparison to Sam's flashy hair, which never bothered me in the least. However, Sam had begged me all day yesterday to join in on her hair appointment and do something "to bring a little fun" to my hair. I finally agreed to think about getting highlights, to which she gave a massive roll of her eyes and began purposefully muttering about "a complete lack of imagination" under her breath, but loud enough for me to hear.

On a whim, more as a prank on Sam than anything else, I got in the chair and asked the hairstylist to color the ends of my hair both silver and a pastel turquoise. I thought after I freaked out Sam that I could have the ends trimmed off in favor of a short hairstyle.

Sam had been speechless when the stylist unveiled my new look. Considering the minimal amount of times that I've witnessed Sam speechless, I grimaced, and turned toward the mirror preparing myself for the worst, pangs of regret already tightening my stomach. I couldn't believe my eyes. It was gorgeous! "Oh. My. Gosh." At last, Sam managed to break free of the shock and stepped forward to run her fingers through my hair, lifting it to get a better look. "I am completely jealous, Piper. It looks amazing on you."

Giving my head a little shake to snap out of the memory, I pointed at the large white van with KDOP Channel 17 News plastered on the side of it. The van had parallel parked at the curb directly in front of our store. While we watched, a lanky teen fumbled with unloading the camera equipment while Missy Sims, the local anchor, sprayed clouds of hairspray on her already perfectly springy curls.

Missy was busy snapping a barrage of orders, pointing all over the place, her hands waving frantically in the air, I think she even stomped her foot once. Nodding to Missy, scrambling to and from the van with all of the equipment, the pale-faced teen quickly began setting up the camera on the sidewalk right in front of our door. Sam and I shared a puzzled look. Closing the pocket knife that I had been using to open boxes of new kitchen utensils, I slipped it into my pocket, wiped the cardboard dust from the gray marble countertops, and grabbed Sam to head outside to investigate.

"Samantha Lowe and Piper Rivers?" Missy asked, jutting the microphone toward me the moment the door swung open.

"I'm Piper, and this is Samantha" I confirmed. "What's going on here?" I wiped sweaty palms on my jeans. Having a camera pointing at our doorway before 7 AM made me more than a little nervous and, I'll admit, a bit abrupt; I couldn't imagine what this might be about.

Samantha, the picture of politeness as always, inquired smoothly, "What can we help you with this morning?"

Completely ignoring Sam, Missy turned to the camera boy, whose name was Pete according to his badge, and made a "rolling" motion with her finger. A small, red light blinked to life on the camera and Missy immediately jumped into her spiel, a wide smile plastered onto her face. "Good morning to all of you early risers. I'm here today with Samantha Lowe and Piper Rivers, the owners of the Ooey-Gooey-Goodness Bakery, and winners of the four-day spa stay at O Heavenly Day Spay."

My mouth dropped open in disbelief.

The O Heavenly Day Spa! We won?!

Sandy Shores Evangelical Church was the largest church in our beachfront town of Seashell Bay. In fact, the church was so massive that there was an entire campus complete with child-care programs, primary school and, of course, the spa.

The spa operated as a spiritual retreat center for both members and numerous women's groups statewide. Often one set of dormitories at the spa was opened to domestic abuse victims or single mothers; they were given jobs and use of the facilities.

It was Sandy Shores Church who sponsored the contest and put up the prize for the Breaking Chains fundraiser, to encourage community members to partner with them in broader ministry opportunities. They donated several weeks a year free of charge to victims of crimes and trafficking or women struggling to get back on their feet after the death of a spouse or divorce.

The spa also accepted paying appointments from members and non-members, as well. Samantha's mother, for one, had weekly appointments booked for months in advance.

Missy turned back to us while I was still processing everything. Samantha nudged me and I slammed my open mouth shut. "What an honor," Samantha placed a hand over her heart and launched into speech mode – a necessary skill as a part of her prestigious family. Did I mention they are one of the original five founding families of Seashell Bay? Or that her father is the mayor? Thankfully, when Samantha spoke she was always genuine; my friend has a heart of gold. "I'm so pleased we were able to come together with local businesses and community members to raise funds and awareness for prevention of such horrific practices…"

I tuned out the conversation, nodding and smiling, knowing Samantha had it covered. I still couldn't believe we won. I thought back to the day the contest had been announced.

~

It was on a regular Sunday afternoon, I was elbow deep in a bowl of batter and barely heard the soft sound of the bell out front announce someone's entry. Sam yelled for me to hurry up front for some exciting news. Samantha almost never yells so, of course, I stopped everything I was doing and hurried out to see what the deal was.

Licking the last bit of cookie dough off of my fingers, I pushed through the white metal door separating the kitchen from the storefront. And I grimaced. Sam's brother, Griffin, stood before the counter.

It wasn't that I had a problem with Griff - not really. He just seemed so uptight sometimes, a hazard of his upbringing I'm sure. Griffin was a building inspector and a by-the-rule-book kind of guy. I just knew I would get a lecture on the health code violations of licking my fingers in a public bakery. He gave me a long look, but to my surprise, the lecture didn't happen.

"Piper, look! There's a contest for local businesses. We just have to enter! It would be a great way to attract more customers and help people, too. Say yes, please?" Sam batted her eyelashes.

I rolled my eyes. "Come on, that face doesn't work on me. Now let me see that paper."

Griffin handed over the flyer that he had been holding up to show Sam. He only slightly raised his eyebrows as I wiped my damp fingers on my jeans, and that might have been a smirk he was trying to hide.

> **Attention Seashell Bay Businesses!**
>
>
>
> March 7 to March 14 will mark our first annual Breaking Chains Fundraiser Contest.
>
> Breaking Chains is an organization for the prevention of and victim support for human trafficking.
>
> The business which raises the most money will send two employees to the O Heavenly Day Spa for a four-day weekend retreat.

Prize donated by Sandy Shores Evangelical Church was printed across the back of the flyer.

~

Missy pulled my attention back to the here and now. "Piper," she began, but I was barely listening.

"Piper, do you have anything you would like to say about this contest or what winning means to you?" Missy waited for my response.

My brain was now kicked into high gear, working on overdrive trying to figure out what to do with the bakery during a four-day absence. Could someone run it for us? Would we need to bake everything before we left? It would really be a shame to miss out on all the new business we had gained from the contest. Then again, I could really use a break and I'd been hearing fantastic rumors about the spa since it opened. Having never been, I have to admit I was more than a little curious.

"Piper?" Missy asked once more.

I willed up a composed smile – I hate public speaking – and tried not to look directly at the camera as I answered, "Thank you for asking Missy. Actually, this fundraiser is very close to my heart. Much too often people think that human trafficking is a third world problem, a problem in poverty-stricken places where nobody is paying attention. The truth is, human trafficking can happen in our very own backyards. And it does."

I paused to collect my breath then carried on, "When I was a child, I lived only a few counties away from here; my best friend Landon and two other children were taken from a school field trip. Eight months later, during a raid on a drug house, several children including Landon were found. One of the girls has never been recovered. After being taken they were forced to work like mules for the gang, kept under the influence of drugs to be easily manipulated, and coerced with threats against their family if they tried to escape."

I think for a moment you could hear crickets in the background. Sam had placed a hand over her heart, unshed tears forming at the corners of her eyes.

Missy, wide-eyed and somewhat stunned but always the consummate professional, recovered in a flash. "Thank you for sharing that grim reminder of why we need to be vigilant and supportive of the organizations such as Breaking Chains whose mission it is to put a stop to such evil." She turned to completely face the camera, blocking Sam and me from further view. "Thanks for tuning in to KDOP Channel 17 News. And now, back to Korina for the weather forecast."

We may as well have dawned our invisibility cloaks at this point. Missy barked orders. Much hustle and bustle began and in no time at all the news van was pulling away from the curb without even a backward glance.

As the proverbial dust cleared, Sam pulled me back into the bakery. "I'm fine, really," I insist over the sound of the tinkling bell on the door.

"Sit down," she said, ignoring my protests like any good friend. "I can't believe you didn't tell me about any of that. I'm getting us some tea and cookies."

Within a minute, Sam settled a heaping plate of Walnut Dark Chocolate cookies on the small table between us. Taking a sip of the delicious iced tea and enjoying a bite of chocolatey-goodness, I knew there was no getting around talking about it now.

"It was a long time ago," I said shrugging. "We were eight. When they found Landon, he had lost around twelve pounds from malnourishment. It was close to a year before he stopped suffering from withdrawals of the drugs that they had been pumping him full of. Three years of counseling. I'm not sure the nightmares ever went away; he moved before we went into junior high."

"That must have been pretty traumatic for you as a kid too, first finding out he was missing and then not understanding why your friend wasn't the same anymore, not being able to help him," Sam said, nodding and encouraging me to continue.

I finished off my second cookie in two giant bites, then took my time wiping crumbs from the table, avoiding looking her in the eyes. "The worst part I think is that sometimes a little part of me still feels guilty. I was home sick that morning and missed the field trip. I cried for weeks after school because I thought that if I had been on the field trip Landon would have been with me and maybe that would have changed things."

"Piper Rivers!" Sam exclaimed and raised an eyebrow. "You know that is not true," she continued emphatically, "your eight-year-old self might have been kidnapped right along with the others for all you know."

"I know, I know. Mom put me in therapy for a month when I told her my feelings. Truly, I do know there is nothing I could have done." I sighed. "The contest flyer was unexpected; it managed to bring each of the painful memories rushing back. And fresh guilt. I don't even know the last time I even thought about Landon; I have no idea where he is or how he's doing now."

"Tell you what," Sam smiled. "Right after our spa retreat, I'll help you search for Landon. He's likely to be on Facebook, Instagram, or some other social media somewhere, almost everyone is, and maybe he is still close by."

Looking at my watch, I stood and hugged my best friend. "Sounds like a plan. But for now, we have to be ready to open in seven minutes so we better hustle." I hurried away, trading the pain and memories for busyness.

~

"Looks like the morning rush is over," Sam called as the tinkling bell announced the exit of yet another satisfied customer.

I could feel the wide grin split my face. The morning rush! I loved the sound of that; it made me so proud of the Ooey-Gooey-Goodness Bakery. Who knew when we started this "irresponsible and childish" business, as Sam's mom Deidra preferred to call it, that it would become popular so quickly? We had opened a little less than a year ago and were already in the black.

It had been a whirlwind of activity ever since the 6 AM broadcast of KDOP's morning news segment airing Missy's impromptu interview of Samantha and me.

Our regulars, the business crowd who came for muffins and scones on the way to the office, congratulated us, of course. Then we had our second unexpected visit of the morning, this time from Mayor Lowe and his PR team to discuss how proud he was of his 'darling daughter taking such a stand against these deplorable crimes against humanity.' She was 'a chip off the old block' and he knew she had a bright future." I was very proud. Samantha didn't roll her eyes once. Until after he left.

A few new faces trickled in as well, some of the retired generations who admitted they had been hesitant to try this "fancy-pants" bakery. One such lady, Mrs. Gladys Hill, was quick to let us know she had been wrong, "I was drinking my coffee this morning, all by myself since my Joe passed on last year, and when I saw you sweet young ladies on the morning news and your kind hearts – well, I just said to myself 'Gladys, you get yourself up and encourage those dear girls to keep doing good and being open-hearted.' So here I am. And now that I've had this scrumptious cinnamon and apple scone, I am especially glad that I listened to my own advice."

There were also some hateful responses to our win. Flo from Flo's flowers almost refused to even speak to me when I went next door to offer her some of our fresh scones, and she did refuse the scones. Before the contest, she would often order three or more a day.

Several of our competitor's friends and family posted rude comments on Facebook, insinuating Sam's family had bought our way into the spa trip. Ha! If only they knew that the mayoral family hadn't even contributed to our bit of fundraising.

Later that morning, Griff came in to snag a to-go bag of cookies, not unusual for him. "Hey sis, nice hair. Has Mother seen it yet?"

"Sadly no," Sam grinned, reaching under the counter for the crisp, white to-go bags. I found myself hoping that one day we could afford bags with our logo. As soon as we committed to a logo. Okay, so probably that day wasn't anytime soon but a girl can dream.

"I need half-a-dozen to go please, whatever is hot," Griff told her. Griff loves dessert.

I was folding napkins with my back to them, closest to the kitchen doors, so it was no surprise to me when Sam turned and asked, "Piper, can you run in the kitchen and grab six of the monster cookies that just came out of the oven?"

Turning to her, I smiled, "Of course, monster cookies for a monstrous appetite coming right up."

"Piper?" I swear Griff's jaw dropped right open. "Your hair...wow! I didn't even recognize you with those colors."

Winking at me, Sam turned back to her brother, "Right! Gorgeous, isn't she?"

"Yes!" Griff nodded, still staring. He blinked, "I mean, it looks nice. Very unique."

Disappearing through the kitchen door I shook my head. I would get Samantha back for that. I didn't know how yet, but somehow, I would. Bagging up the cookies, I returned them to the front. Griff thanked us and headed back to work. We never made him pay; Griff had helped us get a lot of remodel work done and kept us up to code when we were remodeling before our grand opening. He had always been very supportive of his sister, unlike their parents. A few cookies on the house were nothing in return.

Quite possibly the most surprising result from our appearance on the news was our new-found respectability, or at least almost respectability, with Deidra Lowe's Ladies Society. Deidra herself didn't have the time to come, obviously, but she sent her secretary Abigail over instead.

It was around 9:15 AM when Abigail came in, a thick binder in hand.

"Good morning," I greeted her in surprise as Griffin left and I saw her next in line.

"Hi, Abigail. Did I miss an appointment with Mother?" Sam asked.

"Good morning Piper, Samantha. No, nothing like that," she assured us. Abigail was about twenty-one years old, only one year younger than us. She was a bit heavy-set and wore glasses but had a keen fashion sense. Her blonde hair was cut in a cute bob style that I was certain I could never pull off, but it framed her face perfectly. According to Sam, she was very bright; her time was wasted fetching and scheduling for Deidra as far as I was concerned.

I looked at Sam who just shrugged, equally as perplexed as I about what errand Deidra could have sent the poor girl on today.

"I need to place an order for the Ladies Society's brunch tomorrow," Abigail flipped a page on her clipboard and began to reel off a list.

"Wait, what?" I asked in confusion. Never had Deidra so much as tasted a cookie from our bakery. She adamantly refused to support her precious daughter "throwing her life away."

"I'm sorry Abigail, do you mean to tell me my mother actually *wants* to order baked goods? From us? Instead of from The Busy Bee where she has ordered for at least twenty years? And she sent you to do it rather than call and ask me?" Samantha crossed her arms and raised an eyebrow.

Abigail placed two fingers at her temple as if she was getting a headache.

"Call me Abby, please. Yes. I'm sorry. Look, I know it is silly and I tried to tell her she should come and order them herself, that you would be really pleased to see her." She rolled her eyes. "I think that nearly got me fired. So please, let me place the order and do my job. I need the approval and recommendations that working for your mom can get for me, even if working for her may kill me".

I decided right then that we should cut Abby some slack.

"My goodness, I can't imagine the stress that goes with your job. Have you eaten yet?" I asked her.

"Me?" she seemed startled. "Well, um, why no I haven't had time so far. The Ladies are all in a tizzy about the news this morning and not knowing about the business and in shock that Piper is associated with a crime and …"

"Piper is not associated with a crime," Sam jumped in.

"Well, I know that. You know that group just loves gossip."

"My mother is not getting a discount," Sam harrumphed.

Abby laughed out loud.

"Here," I handed over a napkin-wrapped Oatmeal Chocolate Chip Flax Muffin – yes, I know, shocker - occasionally we have healthier options, trust me they are still delicious. "At least have some food while we go over the order for brunch."

The rest of the day was busy but nothing out of the ordinary. However, just before closing up, I discovered a weird and disturbing note underneath of two pennies on one of the corner tables. I didn't know what to make of it so I showed it to Sam.

Printed in bold block letters it read: **YOU CAN'T HAVE EVERYTHING, I'M WATCHING YOU.**

"That is so strange," Sam agreed. "It doesn't even say who it is for; I have no idea unless it could be to us from someone else who's mad that we won the contest?"

"Yeah, maybe." I put the note in my apron pocket as I continued to wipe down tables and did my best to forget all about it.

TWO

"Coffee," Sam groaned. "Must have coffee."

I gulped down my own iced green tea, understanding her need for caffeine. In order to fulfill Deidra Lowe's order on time, we had to do a lot of extra baking and fast. That meant we got to work at three o'clock this morning. Artisan bread for their cheese and sandwiches, four types of scones and three different muffin flavors, plus lemon cookies and almond cookies. I'm not sure how many members there were in the Ladies Society, but they ordered enough baked goods to feed half the elementary school. That was on top of our regular baking for the goodies we would sell in the store today.

Exhaustion was an understatement; I'm certain my appearance alone could rival the walking dead.

"On the bright side," I made for an attempt at positivity, "we won't hurt for profits during our four-day absence thanks to Deidra's order."

"Nope, and if by some miracle they start ordering for even half of their brunches and teas and plethora of meetings from us, then we will be able to afford that second oven sooner than we hoped."

"True. Cheers to larger ovens."

"Cheers!"

I left the last tray of Butterscotch Oatmeal Cookies in the oven for Sam to look after while I went about opening the bakery. I unlocked the door and turned the sign to open, tidied up the counter and flipped the light switches to illuminate the glass display cases full of – you guessed it – ooey-gooey goodness.

Gladys turned up as our first customer of the day.

"Good morning dearies," she greeted warmly. "Remind me, which of you is which now?"

"I'm Samantha, this is Piper," Sam smiled, gesturing to me. "What can we get for you today?"

"A muffin today I think, perhaps blueberry if you have one?"

"Coming right up!"

"Thank you."

"How do you take your coffee?" I asked Gladys as she got comfortable at a small table by the register.

"Dark roast please, with a good helping of cream to cool it down."

Gladys sat at her table most of the morning, accepting a couple of coffee refills and reading her Bible. As the rush slowed, Sam took a plate of cookies over and asked Gladys if she would mind sharing her table during our break.

"For some of those mouth-watering morsels I'd probably share my house," Gladys smiled as soft laugh lines crinkled around her bright eyes. Gladys was easy to talk to and had us holding our sides in laughter in no time as she recounted memories of her husband and their younger days.

After a while, Gladys did grow serious again, however. "I've made a decision today, but I need to know if it is okay with both of you first."

"What is it, Gladys?" I asked curiously, unsure what bearing I should have on this sweet lady's decisions.

"I've been very lonely but chatting with you two feels like having new friends. In my reading over my favorite scriptures this morning I was reminded of how much our good Lord encourages us to rest."

Sam nodded for her to continue.

"I haven't been to that fancy spa at the church yet," Gladys continued, "and even though I don't get out of the house much, it isn't very restful for me. My mind is churning all day but there isn't really anything to do besides vacuum night and day."

I snorted because I can't imagine vacuuming more than two or three times a month, truly.

"I thought, if you didn't mind, I would book a stay at the spa the same four days that you two will be there and we can make a real vacation of it?"

"Oh, how fun Gladys!" Sam said.

"Excellent!" I agreed at the same time.

"Well that settles it," I said raising a cookie in salute.

Knowing me well, Sam raised her own. "To the spa stay vacay!" she said.

The bell tinkled musically and Sam threw a wide smile to the entrance. I rose, preparing to help our next customer.

"Oh. It's you." I said, sitting back down to finish off my cookie.

"How's that for greeting your top taste-tester?" Griff huffed good-naturedly, dragging a chair up to the already packed, round table and straddling it backward. "You've got something right here by the way." And before I knew what was happening, he swiped chocolate from the side of my mouth and licked his finger.

"Oh, hello handsome," Gladys grinned at the exchange. "You must be Piper's boyfriend. I'm Gladys."

"What!" I practically shouted and Sam blew tea out of her nose; I had a brief moment of being thankful she had switched beverages mid-morning because I'm betting hot coffee would have burned a tad more severely.

"Piper has a boyfriend?" Griff's eyebrows furrowed, quite the change from his usual confident expressions.

"Oh! This spa trip is going to be so much fun, I can tell already," Gladys laughed, amused at the tizzy she instigated at our table.

As usual, once composed that is, Sam stepped in with the niceties, "Gladys, I'd like you to meet my brother Griffin."

"Who is not my boyfriend, may I clarify," I told Gladys, my cheeks still feeling a bit warm.

"Pleased to meet you, ma'am," Griff said, laying on the Southern charm.

Saved by the bell, another few customers started trickling in and I hurried to attend them.

Griff didn't stay long. He left to go back to his office across the street after devouring three of his favorite snacks, Dark Chocolate Chip Brown Sugar Cookies, not that I've been paying attention.

The rest of the day passed as normal and before long, Sam was cleaning the kitchen and preparing to close up for the evening. We decided to close early, at 5 PM, so that we had plenty of time to pack for our spa stay.

"I can't believe it's here already."

"Me neither," I agreed.

"I'm excited. I will admit since I strayed from Mother's good graces, I have missed having a good massage; she goes every week you know."

"I don't know, I'm not too keen on the idea of strangers touching me. Still, I'm glad for a break and I think it will be fun for Gladys to be there with us."

"She is a character, isn't she? I can't believe she went skinny dipping with her husband on their 40th anniversary!"

"I'm guessing that is probably one of the numerous reasons your mother doesn't include her in," I raised my nose in the air and gave my best upper-class refined accent, "the Seashell Bay Ladies Society activities." Sam doubled over in hysterics.

I laughed too. Deidra really was too easy to laugh at, mostly because she took herself so seriously.

Grabbing the broom while Sam started stacking chairs onto tables, I did a quick lap around the front of the store. I emptied the dustpan into the trash sack by the back door, tying the strings up so it could be hauled to the dumpster we shared with our neighbors on this little shopping strip – Flo's Flowers, Auntie Em's Antiques, and the Bait & Tackle store.

"That looks like everything," said Sam, joining me and grabbing her keys from the hook on the side of one cabinet.

"Great, I'll take the trash. See you tomorrow morning."

"Yeah – I'll pick you up at 6?"

"Perfect!"

Sam locked the back door as I strode to the dumpster to deposit our offering. By the time I clicked the unlock button on my key fob, Samantha's yellow Nissan Juke was speeding out of the rear parking lot. Climbing into my dark blue four-door pickup truck, I crossed my fingers that it would crank. Bought from a used car lot three years ago, it had almost two hundred thousand miles on it and lately seemed to cough and sputter more than it used to. Still, it was mine, free and clear, and I loved it. I loved to drive down on the beach, park and put the tailgate down. I could just sit and watch the ocean for hours. Tonight, the truck roared to life and I said a quick prayer of thanks before driving home.

~

Two hours later I flopped onto the couch with a sigh of frustration. What in the world was I supposed to pack for a spa trip? I've never been to a spa…who am I kidding I've never even had my nails done. I was stressing out way too much over this, which meant maybe I was more nervous about leaving the bakery for almost a week than I thought I was. It was a vacation; vacation would be nice. I just need to figure out what specifically to pack and be done thinking about it.

I knew what I needed to do. Snatching my phone off the turquoise coffee table, I dialed Sam. When the ringing ceased, I started rambling before she could even say hello. "What in the world am I supposed to pack for a spa stay? What are we even going to be doing – how do I know what is appropriate? I mean how many clothes do we even need? I thought they made you be naked or wear a towel or something to get a massage? Can we really spend four days getting a massage; I'll lose my mind."

A distinctly masculine throat cleared on the other end of the phone.

I checked the screen. It said Sam I Am, my contact name for Samantha, so at least I had dialed the right number.

"Sam?"

"Nope."

I slapped a palm to my forehead. Just what I was afraid of.

"Griff."

"Yep." More throat clearing.

"Why the heck would you be answering Sam's phone?" I shouted, embarrassed that he had been the recipient of my brief freak out and embarrassing lack of clothes discussion.

"I'm having dinner with Sam. She went to the restroom and left her phone. I thought something might be wrong when I saw it was you, so I answered."

"Nope, nothing wrong here."

"That isn't what it sounded like to me."

"You heard wrong."

"So, about those spa clothes..." he started in a low voice.

I heard some background noises and what might have been light screeching and laughter.

"Piper," Sam's voice came through the speaker. "Sorry, I had to wrestle the phone from my about-to-get-no-free-desserts-ever-again big brother. He said you needed some help with something?"

"Never mind, I got it," I lied, pretty sure I could feel my face glowing red for the second time today.

"Okay, you sure?"

"I'm sure. Thanks, Sam, I've gotta go."

I threw the phone onto the couch cushions and jumped up. What in the world was up with today and embarrassing moments in front of Griff? I had never cared what he thought before. I put a chamomile tea pod into the Keurig and marched to my bedroom, determined to pack and go to bed.

Beep.

Beep. Beep.

Faintly, I could hear my text messages going off in the living room. Tossing the two pair of yoga pants and cargo pants that I was holding into my lime and turquoise chevron duffle bag on my way out of the bedroom, I hurried to read them.

Sam: Made Griff spill.

Sam: Comfy clothes.

Sam: And one or two cute dresses.

I hit reply.

Me: Why dresses??

Me: Really?

Sam: Yes. They have fancy meals at these places sometimes.

Me: And they don't think you can eat meals in yoga pants?

Sam: lol lol lol!

Sam: Just bring one or two. Can borrow some of mine also.

Me: Fine.

My tea finished making in the small kitchen alcove of my apartment. I poured it into a large mug, adding a few ice cubes. What? I'm from the south, we don't drink hot tea.

After several fortifying sips, I felt calm enough to face my arch nemesis: my closet.

It isn't that I didn't enjoy or have clothes. I did. I just leaned more towards comfortable, practical clothes. Unlike Sam's mom, my mom wasn't a fancy dress-up kind of person. My parents both worked long hospital and nursing shifts. They wore scrubs by day and shorts by night. I guess I kind of adopted the "if you don't need it, don't buy it" habit and the majority of the time, I didn't need to dress up.

Fortunately for my closet's sake, when Sam and I became friends during college a few years ago, she had taken me shopping with her several times. Not because she had a problem with my style. She just loved to shop. I knew somewhere in this mess were at least two or three dresses Sam had bought me a while ago. Now, I just had to find them. And hope they still fit, I thought, acknowledging the niggling fear that maybe I'd consumed too much cookie dough lately.

Wrenching hanger after hanger of t-shirt, jeans, and the occasional sweater out of the way I finally succeeded.

"Gotcha!" I triumphed over the closet too soon; as it mocked me in silence, the hanger that I needed snagged on several others sending everything to the floor in a jumbled mess.

Forty-five minutes and an entire closet reorganizing session later, I had my duffle zipped up tight and tossed it by the door. Surely, I wasn't going to need any more than that for only four days, and I was staying in the same town too!

A shower and a shave later – can't have people rubbing and massaging stubbly legs after all – I pulled down the covers on my bed and crawled in.

Knowing I had several hours to sleep late in the morning compared to a normal bakery day, I opened my nightstand drawer and dug around until I found my Kindle e-reader. There was a particularly handsome knight wandering around lost in a forest where he stumbled upon a maddeningly bossy maiden who refused to believe she needed to be rescued. It had been weeks since I had taken the time to read; typically, I spent all my free time making up new recipes. Tonight, however, I vowed to begin my relaxing early and I was more than ready to find out whose stubbornness won out at the end of this hilarious tale.

THREE

Beep.

Thirty seconds after I closed my eyes my phone went off.

Except the phone said 6:05 AM, which would mean I had truly slept a full seven hours. Wow. When was the last time that happened, I wondered?

Beep.

It was a new message from Sam: I'm outside.

Sam: I brought the last three chocolate chip muffins.

I pulled on my socks before hopping out of bed and shuffling to unlock the front door of my tiny condo.

"Morning!" I hugged my best friend, then opened the door for her to come in.

"Piper, did you actually oversleep?" her eyes twinkled. I was known for being up before the alarm could even think of going off back when we were in college. She said the only reason she didn't starve was that I got bored and cooked breakfast every day while waiting for the alarm to sound and signal the "start" of the day.

"Technically, it isn't oversleeping if there was no alarm set."

"Ha. If you say so," she rolled her eyes. "Go get dressed, I'll heat these up."

"Thanks. Your coffee pods are in the drawer."

It didn't take me long to become presentable. I'm not a primping and preening type of girl so some snug black slacks and a flowy silver top, plus two short French braids later I was back in the kitchen scarfing down my share of the muffins.

Samantha, who please remember would probably look gorgeous in a neon purple bag, wore an understated gray jumpsuit and red, dangly feather earrings that matched her hair which was in a sleek bun at the nape of her neck.

"By the way," Sam said over her shoulder as she rinsed her coffee cup, "I told Gladys we could swing by and pick her up as well."

"Great. Where does she live?"

"The address she gave me is very close to Sandy Shores Evangelical Church so it will be on the way. You ready?"

I swept a lightning-quick glance around: lights were off, sink devoid of dishes, bag waiting by the door, thermostat switched to conserve energy.

"Yeah, I think I'm ready. Let's get this over with," I grouched, tossing my keys and wallet into a side pocket of the duffle.

Sam snickered, "It is a spa Piper, not a torture chamber."

"Whatever you say," I rolled my eyes.

The drive to pick up Gladys was a scenic one. Her home was in a small residential retirement community only two blocks from the beach. Bungalow homes, all of a cookie-cutter style similarity but in different shades of color, lined two clean, quiet streets. A canary-yellow bungalow screamed for attention, standing out from the muted pink, tan, blue and green hues sported by the neighboring homes.

"Let me guess…" I said as Sam drove in the direction of the exceptionally bright bungalow.

"Yep," she said. "Number 374. This is Gladys." She pulled the car into the short, cement drive and parked.

"I think your car blends in with the house," I joked.

As we walked toward the door, Sam stopped and put a hand on my arm.

"Do you hear that?"

"Yes. Sounds like Gladys is in the back yard."

The voice carried softly on the breeze over the fence but the words were indistinguishable.

"Look, there's a gate," I pointed.

Sam nodded and we walked the five or six feet to the gate in the fence. I raised my hand to knock on it but paused as the conversation out back amplified.

"Behave yourself while I'm gone, do you understand?"

I didn't hear any response but Gladys continued speaking as if there had been.

"Good. It will only be a few days you know. And watch your brother, too."

Odd. Surely Gladys didn't have children living at home who needed caring for?

Sam looked at me and shrugged.

Curiosity aroused, I rapped my knuckles on the gate which bounced under the pressure, flinging the latch loose.

"Hello?" Gladys called, leaning around the corner of the bungalow. "Oh, hello, Piper, Samantha. Come on back here."

"We didn't mean to interrupt," Sam said as she walked through the gate and glanced behind Gladys.

I nearly ran into her as she stopped short and tilted her head.

Looking past Sam, I could see that Gladys was alone. That was strange.

"No need to apologize. You weren't interrupting. Old Jack here isn't much for conversation anyway." Gladys smiled and patted a tall, thin palm tree.

With a face.

"Oh!" I understood now why Sam had stopped walking suddenly.

Carved into the palm, just about eye-level, were two eyes and a grinning mouth. Gladys patted the tree affectionately, her smile softening as she looked at it and then back at us.

"Jack?" Sam asked as Gladys led us to a round table and chairs where lemonade was ready to pour into glasses of melting ice.

Gladys poured us each a glass of lemonade and sat down. "I needed a friend after my Harold passed away. My neighbor suggested I go with her to the Senior Center and do some painting class to meet new people. Well, I wasn't much for painting and I wasn't much for listening to a bunch of whiners which is all I think the class was really good for so I left about halfway through. On my way out though, a sign on the bulletin board caught my eye. It was for a wood carving class the following Saturday."

Gladys took a sip of her lemonade and checked her watch.

"Oh my! We best be going. I don't want to make us late to the spa."

Three garment bags, three! And a suitcase plus toiletries bag later, we had Gladys loaded into the car and were on our way to the spa, at last.

"Come on," I told Gladys.

"Yeah, you can't just leave us hanging in the middle of a story like that," Sam insisted. "Tell us about the wood carving class and Jack."

"Oh, alright. I went to the woodcarving class the next weekend. Turns out, I have a real knack for it. We carved some small logs into rough dolphins."

"No way!" I said, truly amazed. That would be such a cool talent. Not that I had anywhere to apply wood carving but cool nonetheless.

"And did you make new friends that weekend, too?" Sam asked as she stopped at a four-way stop. The spa was straight in front of us now, though still a few miles away.

"No. The class was full of men young enough to be my children except for one or two old geezers who thought they could sweet talk me into splitting the Senior Citizen Supper Special at Denny's. No, thank you on that deal."

I coughed into my hand to cover my laughter. Sam met my eyes in the rearview mirror and I could tell keeping a straight face was nearly killing her but since she was driving there wasn't much else that she could do about it.

"I got up the next day," Gladys continued without giving our mirth a second glance, "and I went out back to see if I could find some driftwood. There wasn't anything close by. I leaned on the palm tree, just thinking about life, and started talking out loud. I do that sometimes. Then it hit me, I could carve my good friend and best listener a face. So, I did. Jack was the first but he is always happy. That is a lot of pressure. I needed someone around that was maybe a little grumpy, too, so I wouldn't feel so out of place if I were grumpy. I planted Drew next to Jack. He's a stubby little thing right now, kind of jealous of Jack, and so he got to have the grumpy face."

Boy, Gladys wasn't kidding about being lonely I thought to myself.

"I think I need to see Drew when we take you home, Gladys. I must have missed him today," Sam told her.

"Look! We're here," I leaned forward from the back seat and pointed to the white gravel lined driveway to the O Heavenly Day Spa. All thoughts of Gladys talking to trees vanished as my jaw dropped open at the opulent spread where we would be spending the next four days.

FOUR

I stepped out of the car and continued to stare in awe. The spa was so much more impressive up close than it had appeared from the highway.

From a distance, it looked to be a cute but oversized house.

Now, staring at it, the word that came to mind was splendor. The building was a pale, moss green which stood out in relief against the blue ocean and white sands just in the background. Tan Spanish clay tiles on the roof added a charm all their own, not to mention the arches used everywhere in the architecture, from the tall arch above the front steps to the windows all framed out in arches at the top. I couldn't even begin to imagine what custom glass for those must have cost.

Three young men, tastefully attired in matching tan pants and white button-down shirts, appeared at the car and effortlessly hauled our luggage into the foyer.

Tile floors sparkled in welcome as we stepped into the beautiful building. Ceiling fans with blades in the shape of giant palm leaves circulated blessedly cool air. I was intrigued by the fans, not only for their artistic design, but for the way they spun in a floor to ceiling direction instead of round and round as one would expect a typical fan to do.

Samantha returned from the check-in desk, already having filled out the paperwork while I was absorbed in my fascination with the fans, and she was accompanied by one of the porters.

"Please, follow me. A small respite has been prepared for you in the Tea Room," he informed as he led us a short distance down the hall.

A very short while later, I glared at the blobs sitting on the plate in front of me, both minuscule and suspiciously slimy. We were sitting in the Tea Room, an expansive waiting lounge decorated as if a tea party was going to bust out at any minute; we were served tiny excuses for "food" on delicate china plates that might break if you looked at them too hard. No way was I touching any of this.

"Not torture, you say?" I said with more snark than was perhaps needed. "What precisely do you call this, please do tell me?"

Sam didn't have an opportunity to respond as Gladys mistook my sarcasm literally, assuming I was asking a genuine question.

"Pardon me, ma'am?" Gladys signaled a serving girl passing by. "What do you call this stuff again?"

"Hors-d'oeuvres," the girl supplied before moving quickly away.

"There you are Piper," Gladys smiled as she selected three or four olives, a devil-egg spread toast, caviar, snails (I don't care if they do sound fancy as "escargot" – they are super slimy snails, period), and what appeared to be a small portion of cheese-stuffed zucchini. "Of course, in my day, I think we would have just called them finger foods."

Sam crunched on a grilled veggie bruschetta and shrugged.

My stomach rumbled. "Please tell me there will be real food at some point during our stay? Otherwise, I may starve."

"These are only the pre-pampering snacks, come on Piper you are going to love this place. I promise."

My retort was prevented by the entrance of the concierge.

"Miss Lowe, Mrs. Hill, and Miss Rivers?" The short, slim man addressed them. He had dark hair, and perfectly trimmed eyebrows, which he raised expectantly while the rest of his face remained impassive.

We stood. "Yes, that's us," I spoke up, more than happy to leave the hors-d'oeuvres behind.

Broussard, according to the thin white name badge, escorted us back to the reception lobby in the next room where Sam had signed in, given our names and been asked to wait while our "personal assistants" were finishing with their current guests.

I focused my attention back on the room in front of me, which boasted its own elegant beauty, though in a more modern style. Now, aside from Broussard and the chipper Mika who had taken our names earlier, three other staff members were awaiting us in reception.

"Mrs. Hill," Broussard motioned her forward, "as part of the VIP package, Lola will be your personal assistant for the duration of your stay." With a nod, the young girl he indicated stepped forward and smiled widely at Gladys.

"Good morning Lola," Gladys graced her with the same warm and welcoming smile that I was coming to know her for.

"Ma'am," Lola nodded. "Allow me to take your things." Purse and sweater were whisked from Gladys in seconds amidst protests that she wasn't so old and frail as to not be able to hold a bag yet. Broussard had to step in and insist that as a guest who purchased a VIP stay the staff were required to provide the utmost service. Reprimanded, Gladys huffed and followed Lola to her suite at last.

"Miss Lowe," Broussard continued as if not bothered in the least, "your assistant is one of our best and you should find her more than competent to see to any and everything you need. The smallest request is her pleasure. Margarite," again with the head nodding. Broussard and his stuffy manners were already on my nerves.

"Senorita Lowe," the beautiful older Hispanic woman, probably in her sixties, bowed so low to Sam that I was afraid her hair might drag the floor. My guess was, the spa was trying to emphasize that Sam received the best service because they couldn't afford for complaints to be brought to Deidra Lowe, one of their most frequent customers. Little did they know, Sam wasn't much of the complaining type.

As with Gladys, Samantha allowed herself to be led from reception down a wide hallway to a suite somewhere in the facility.

"Please, enjoy your stay," Broussard inclined his head to Sam as she passed, all deference.

Now it was my turn.

"Ah, yes, Miss Rivers," Broussard brushed his eyes quickly over me and I couldn't help feeling as if I had been found lacking, "as one of our contest winners, VIP treatment is included for you as well. Jill will assist you."

Without so much as a goodbye or a farewell, Broussard spun, clicking his feet together and striding resolutely away. It was very clear where I was seen on the guest list. I wondered what Broussard thought of all the times the spa was opened up for free to the less fortunate such as human trafficking victims. It was after all partially run as a business and partially a part of the church used for ministry to those who would never be able to afford a luxury like this. I bet that didn't make him very happy at all.

Jill broke into my thoughts and I dismissed Broussard as easily as he dismissed me, "Miss Rivers, would you care to follow me, please?"

"I will not follow you," I said.

"Oh…" Jill's eyes widened and she looked around for help.

"I will not follow you," I continued, "unless you will call me Piper," I grinned.

Jill smiled and laughed, immediately at ease again." Happily!" she agreed. I let her take my bag and we set off down the same hallway as my friends.

"Tell me, Jill, how long have you worked at O Heavenly Day Spa?"

"Three months."

"Do you know if my room will be near Sam and Gladys?" I chewed on my bottom lip, hoping it would be and avoiding the anxiety crowding in at being on my own in this enormous place where I felt I didn't belong, like a big rubber clown nose trying to pass as a tomato.

"Yes. You each have one of our VIP suites. They are in their own wing and are connected to each other by an adjoining sitting room."

"A sitting room?"

"Yes, that is correct."

"A room for sitting? My word how fancy is this place!"

Jill turned and winked, "Fancy-schmancy."

I laughed. "Oh, we are going to get along great," I told her. Perhaps this wasn't going to be as bad as I feared. At least Jill had a sense of humor and I would be close to Sam and Gladys.

We arrived at the suite, which was at the end of possibly the world's longest hallway. At least if I got lost the entrance was in a straight line from my room, even if it was on the opposite side of the building. Jill opened the door and we entered into the sitting room first; I simply stood and stared.

Embossed gold wallpaper reflected the low chandeliers, making the room bright. I counted three deep purple divans for reclining. Cozied up to a fireplace, snug as could be, were four plush purple wing-back chairs with delicate gold roses embroidered into the cushions; all of the furniture looked plush enough that you might sink into them forever should you sit there. The carpeting was so thick I was literally itching to toss off my shoes and socks this very second to curl my toes up in it.

To my left was a floor to ceiling bookshelf full of devotionals, Bibles, word searches and who knows what else, I didn't take the time to inspect it.

There were three doors, one on each of the other walls. From the door on the left, Sam emerged, took one look at me and burst out laughing.

I gave myself a tiny shake, certain my mouth may have dropped open while I was taking in the magnificence of this sitting room.

Jill entered the room on my left with my bag and returned empty-handed so I knew that must be my suite. I decided I could explore it later.

"Ladies," she smiled. "Is there anything else I can get for you at this moment?"

"No thank you," Sam answered for us both. "Margarite left us the spa services menus and said we have about an hour to decide and turn in our order?"

"Yes. I hope you have a wonderful time. Piper, my room is down the hall and there is an intercom by your bed and here by the fireplace. Please page if you need anything at all, my number is three. I will also escort you to each of your services once you are ready."

"Great – thanks, Jill!"

After she exited, Sam and I threw ourselves onto one of the divans giggling. "I am so going to be mega-underdressed for this place," I told her.

Gladys appeared from the last door at that moment wearing a fluffy white robe. "Piper dear, I plan to be underdressed for the next four days." Which of course threw us into another fit of laughter.

I saw several papers spread out on the ornate glass and gilded coffee table. Giving in, I rid myself of my shoes and socks and eased down to sit cross-legged in front of the tables.

"Sam," I raised puzzled eyes, "what kind of menus are these? There isn't any food on here at all."

Gladys chuckled.

Sam was very patient with me as she explained, "The spa offers several types of services, a few include massage or manicure or steam, and many of the services have different options too. So, we choose from the menus what we want. We literally place an order for pampering!"

I scanned a few of the menus in front of me:

Heavenly Massage Menu
- Hot Stone Massage
- Deep Tissue Massage
- Full Body Massage
- Reflexology Foot Massage
- Tension Release Neck Massage

Heavenly Manicure Menu
- French Manicure
- Gel Nails
- Hot Wax Dip
- Deluxe Manicure and Nail Painting
- Bejeweled Nails

Heavenly Relaxation Menu
- Jacuzzi
- Steam Room
- Dry Sauna

- Meditation and Silent Reflection
- Yoga
- Seaweed Wrap
- Chocolate Mask

The list went on and on. There were additional details shown beside each service. Several notated that a group or individual option were both available; others, like meditation, were for individuals only.

Passing the menus up to Gladys and Sam on the couch, I shook my head in amazement. I hadn't realized places this deluxe even existed for most of my life, and I never in a million years imagined I would be in one. It was almost unreal.

"You pick," I told Sam feeling more than a little overwhelmed.

"Why don't we each pick a few things?" ever the diplomat, she just couldn't help it. Sam passed the pedicure menu to Gladys, the relaxation menu back to me, and mulled over one of the others herself.

"Don't forget, whatever we don't try today we can do tomorrow or the next day girls," Gladys was giddy with excitement. To be honest, her enthusiasm was more than a little contagious.

"Okay, I vote Steam Room and Chocolate Mask today."

"Sounds great, Piper," Sam agreed. "I think the Foot Massage and the Jacuzzi should make the list also."

"Your turn Gladys."

"Well let's see here. The Deluxe Pedicure; it comes with a sugar scrub and a hot towel wrap."

"Perfect!" Sam beamed.

I stood and made my way to the intercom by the fireplace, but before I could push three for Jill number two lit up and Margarite's voice filtered through.

"Hola ladies, por favor, Senorita Lowe you are ready to place your selection?" Margarite asked in her broken English, her r's coming out in a beautiful rolling Spanish accent.

Sam hustled to the intercom beside me, rolling her eyes as I mouthed 'creepy'. "Yes Margarite, we are all ready, gracias."

The intercom light blinked off.

"What, are they listening in on us? You know that was strange, I was just about to push the button." I insisted to Sam.

She shrugged off my discomfort, "They are trained to be efficient. We have had plenty of time to look over the menus you know."

Moments later, there was a light tapping on the door. It opened before the tapping even stopped and in came all three of our personal assistants with clipboards in hand.

We placed our requests and, after a moment of conferring, the ladies sorted out a schedule that allowed us to stay together for everything but the steam room and the jacuzzi. Gladys decided to have quiet meditation instead of the steam, saying she would use that time for her Bible study today.

We would begin with the foot massage, followed by the chocolate-mask facial together. Afterward, Gladys would go to her room for her quiet time while Sam and I split up for the steam room and jacuzzi, alternating afterward. Jill chimed in that by that time the late lunch would be served in the outdoor garden. Sam, Gladys, and I agreed to meet up there after changing clothes.

When lunch was finished, we would venture to the nail salon for our pedicures together before retiring to our room to dress for dinner. I was still dying to see an actual food menu, but there just wasn't time to hunt one down.

Our assistants, it felt so odd thinking of them that way, left to turn in our schedules so that the services could be prepped. "If you would prefer to change into more comfortable clothes, we will return for you in ten minutes to escort you to the massage wing," Jill told us as she went out, closing the door behind her.

"I'm quite cozy," Gladys grinned cheekily, still lounging in the fluffy robe. I noticed it had clouds embroidered on the front with 'O Heavenly Day' underneath. Good. That meant she found it in her suite and I probably had one in my room too. I looked forward to slipping it on after dinner this evening.

Sam and I changed in less than fifteen minutes, both coming out in loose cargo pants and tank tops. We had discovered fluffy white flip-flop house shoes in our rooms and tossed those on as well. I offered to get Gladys hers from her room but she declined. "Can't stand those things between my toes. I'll wear my own shoes but thank you."

Right on schedule, more light tapping on the door preceded the return of Lola, Margarite, and Jill.

"If everyone is ready, por favor, this way." Margarite gestured to the hallway.

Gladys rubbed her hands together in glee, "Let's get this party started!"

Sam and I chuckled and fell in step behind everyone.

FIVE

The room we were taken to for our foot massage was about midway down the hall from our suites, back in the direction of the reception area. It was beautifully decorated with a calming water theme. Fountains. Streams. Babbling brooks. Each of the four walls was a mural of indescribable beauty. The room itself was divided in half by a six-inch wide live river meandering along the floor.

There were eight chairs set up in the room, four on each side of the river. Two of the chairs were occupied so we were led to three chairs on the vacant half of the room. The chairs were firm yet comfortable, and after we seated ourselves Margarite nodded to Lola who pushed a button on each chair sending us into a deep reclining position and elevating our feet.

Jill, in the meantime, removed our shoes and slid them onto discreet shelves below the chairs.

"We return for you in thirty minutes." Margarite preceded the other assistants from the room.

Three men came in through a different entrance behind us. Two were close to mine and Sam's age if I had to guess and the last one, I would estimate in his fifties. With a clap of his hands, the older gentleman dimmed the can lights above our chairs. I turned to raise my eyebrows at Sam but she was laying back with her eyes shut, completely relaxed from what I could tell.

Soft, trickling water sounds began playing low in the background. I laid back, finding myself lulled deeper into relaxation when both hands of the man at my feet applied deep pressure and began rhythmically working over each and every muscle from my toe to my calf. Who knew one could derive so much pleasure from a foot rub!

I blinked and opened my eyes, surprised to find the room brightly lit yet again and the men gone. Evidently, judging by my heavy and sleep-crusted lids, I had dozed off. Sam too was stretching in her chair, but Gladys was missing.

The door from the hallway swung open revealing Margarite, Lola, and Jill. Gladys shuffled in behind them.

"Had to use the restroom," she explained.

Each of our personal assistants reached under our respective chairs. Margarite slipped shoes onto Sam's feet. Gladys wiggled hers in front of Lola. The poor woman evidently didn't pay attention to Gladys already in full footwear, and Lola ceased her attempt to find shoes under the chair. Jill continued to dig underneath of my own.

"What's wrong Jill?" I asked as her movements became a bit more frantic, jostling the last of my sleepiness away.

"Your shoes. Piper, your shoes are gone."

I joined Jill on the floor for the search and expanded it beyond the chair; however, there was no doubt that my fluffy white slippers had disappeared from the room. As we inclined the chair back to its original position, a piece of paper fluttered to the ground. I picked it up and stuck it in my pocket to throw away later.

"Here Piper, you can wear my shoes." Bless Sam's heart, she knew me well enough to know I couldn't stand walking around barefoot on tile and hard flooring.

"Are you sure?" I asked.

She grinned mischievously as she brought them close to me and spoke in a low whisper, assumedly so Margarite couldn't overhear, "Absolutely. Imagine how scandalized my dear mother will be to learn I've been gallivanting around the place barefoot."

Laughing in agreement, I happily slipped the borrowed fluffy flip flops on and looked up, only to find Margarite gazing at us with a stern expression wrinkling her brows.

"Miss Lowe, I order you another shoe right away; come, we no be late to facial," Margarite's accent thickened as she grew more agitated.

As it turned out, Sam didn't have to walk barefoot very far. The facial area was just three doors down a short hallway perpendicular to what I was coming to consider the main hall. We were seated in a small alcove and handed clipboards with waivers to fill out and sign. I started to skim it, but come on, they were just going to stick some chocolate on my face and wipe it off right? With a flick and a swish, I hastily signed my life away before I had time to rethink that decision.

Sam too signed without hesitation, whether because, like me, she was willing to risk it or because she had read the form hundreds of times before and knew what it contained, I have no idea. We had barely turned in our clipboards when Margarite re-appeared around the corner, fluffy white slippers in hand.

"Thank you," Sam dutifully placed the slippers on her feet.

"Maybe it is for the best," I consoled her about the loss of scandalous material for her mother to hear about. "We do want Deidra to place more orders with us remember?"

"Fine," Sam pouted.

At last, Gladys finished painstakingly pouring over her form. She slowly scratched her signature across the bottom and we were all ready to begin.

The door across the hall from our little alcove opened; a young blonde woman smiled, "Welcome! Who's ready for some chocolate?" she joked.

"Me!" they all laughed, but I was completely serious. I should have dipped into my emergency snack stash before we left our suite earlier. Or perhaps I should consider snacking less at the bakery all day so that my body doesn't think that I'm starving to death when I go two hours without food...nope, probably not going to happen, someone has to quality control check the goodies after all.

Thanks to my inner conversation with myself, Gladys and Sam were already in the room. The blonde stood with a puzzled look on her face, likely wondering if I was going to sit out there all day, take off and raid the kitchens for chocolate, or come in for my facial as planned.

Rising I smiled and shrugged, trying to reassure her with my eyes that I was not going to attack her and take away the chocolate.

Instead of an opulently themed room, there was a very organized, clinical vibe here, softened by a few bouquets of flowers on side tables. Furniture was sparse; three chairs reminiscent of those found in a dentist office were spaced about four feet apart. Two of them Gladys and Sam had already climbed onto – still clothed I was relieved to see – and the blonde began working on situating a small neck pillow underneath them to bring maximum comfort.

After she had inserted a u-shaped neck pillow behind each of us and reclined the chairs flat, she introduced herself. Personally, I felt introductions would have made more sense to do when we could look at her and not while we were staring straight at the ceiling. Oh well, not my spa, not my rules.

"Good morning, my name is Jan. I'm a licensed esthetician and have been doing facials at the spa just over two years now. I understand that two of you ladies own a bakery?"

Attempting to nod assent, I knocked my neck pillow loose and poor Jan had to come re-adjust it. "Sorry," I mumbled, embarrassed.

Jan seamlessly continued, "You both work magic with chocolate on a daily basis, but today I'm going to use chocolate in a whole new way. Today I'm going to use a new recipe with chocolate on your skin. Usually, I have an assistant but they have the day off so today it will just be me."

"Can you explain why putting it on our skin is so helpful? I mean, it just seems like a waste of perfectly edible chocolate to me." I couldn't help it. I wanted to know.

Jan smiled, "Great question. A store-bought chocolate mask probably isn't something you want to put on your face. They often contain small particles of either salt or sugar; those jagged particles can actually scratch the surface of your skin. The masks I will be using for your facial treatments today are homemade from only two ingredients: dark cocoa powder and plain yogurt. The lactic acid contained in yogurt helps to unclog dirty pores; the cocoa powder is packed full of flavanols and antioxidants which help protect your skin from UV rays as well as improve blood flow."

"Wow Piper, we have cocoa and yogurt at the bakery. Maybe on slow days, we should indulge in chocolate a bit differently," Sam said.

"Let's get started, shall we?" Jan gathered her already mixed masks and got to work.

Being without an assistant necessitated that Jan applies each of our masks one at a time. Having just napped, unintendedly, during our divine foot massage, and yes, I had to admit I could understand the draw of a good foot massage now, I was restless laying on the table awaiting my turn.

I cut my eyes sideways, straining to watch Jan mix up the chocolate concoction and slather it on my friends but couldn't see much through my peripheral vision besides a portion of one table and my nose. Scared to move and knock off the pillow again, I resigned myself to the ever-exciting activity of counting ceiling tiles.

Seventy-six.

Seventy-seven.

Seventy-eight.

"Alright, Miss Rivers." In the midst of my counting, Jan's face appeared looming large directly over mine. Yelping, I jumped, my head colliding with her nose.

"I'm so, so sorry!" I rubbed my head while apologizing to the poor lady.

Jan, apparently a free bleeder, grabbed a hand towel from a rack nearby and fled the room. Sitting up I put my face in my hands; I am obviously not cut out for the spa life of the rich and fabulous.

Jill must have been stationed nearby to escort us after the facial because it wasn't long at all before she stepped inside. "I saw Jan. What on earth happened?"

"What do you mean?" Sam asked as Gladys cupped her hands to her ears, smearing the chocolate mask.

"What, what did you say?" Gladys asked.

Neither had seen my graceful catastrophe, even now they were unable to open their eyes due to cucumber slices protecting them from the thick chocolate mixture covering their faces which ran their hairline down to the tips of their chins. Gladys's left cucumber was now sliding, making tracks down her cheekbone.

I rolled my eyes and returned my attention to Jill. "There was a small mishap where Jan nearly gave me a heart attack and I, hopefully, did not break her nose, and to top it off I've completely lost count of the ceiling tiles." I laid back down with a sigh.

SIX

Sam and I bid Gladys goodbye as she followed Lola back to our set of suites.

Margarite clapped her hands to hurry us along and preceded us down the hall, back in the direction of the main hall. "I can't remember, which of us is going to the jacuzzi first?" I asked.

Jill answered me, "I am taking you to the jacuzzi. Sam will go to the steam room."

"We get twenty minutes in each," Sam continued, "and then we switch."

"You must shower between," Margarite's thick accent cut into our conversation from several paces in front of us; that woman must have the hearing of bats.

Margarite came to a halt without warning and gestured for us to go into the room to our right. She and Jill followed us inside where Jill explained the obvious. "This is the changing room and locker storage."

"Thanks, Sherlock," I quipped, receiving an elbow from Sam for my trouble.

"Your suits are in the lockers," Jill opened one to reveal my navy blue and pink striped bikini. Okay, not so sure how I feel about someone unpacking my suitcase for me. I looked to Sam but she was already carrying her own yellow and orange Hawaiian flower-print swimsuit to a changing room. Must be normal procedure, I mentally shrugged.

Once changed and wrapped in fluffy robes, also courtesy of the magic lockers, we stepped into the hall to find Margarite and Jill waiting for us.

"This way," Margarite took off again. Talk about a woman on a mission. This time we again went towards the room where our facials, and partial facials, had taken place but took an immediate right turn down yet another offshoot hallway.

Forget menus, I needed a map! I understood the necessity of playing follow the leader in this place with the personal assistants now. The art on the walls were beautiful fluffy cloudscapes and soft sunrises. Viewpoints were both from the ground and aerial. They were breathtaking.

There was a door on each side of the hallway and, as we passed them, I read the gold-scrolled letters on the doors. Seaweed Wrap was on one in large golden letters, Massage labeled the other. At the end of the hall was a long corridor, but instead of turning left or right down the corridor we passed straight across to the continuing hallway on the other side. It was there that we found a door to the steam room on our right and the jacuzzi on our left. A long bar on the walls by each door had hooks.

"Place your robes here please," Jill indicated the hooks.

Margarite hung up Sam's robe for her as I placed my own on the rack. "We return in twenty minutes to switch," Margarite told Sam as she handed her a small porcelain bowl of goop.

After Margarite and Jill were out of earshot, I asked Sam, "What is that gunk she just handed you?"

"It's an exfoliating scrub," Sam said, sniffing the bowl. "This one is honey and sugar, I think. Here smell."

It smelled delicious, causing my stomach to growl. "Why do they keep rubbing food on us?" I groaned. "When do we get to eat it?"

Sam's laughter continued as she entered the steam room. Turning back to the frosted glass door marked Jacuzzi, I pushed it open, peering cautiously through the crack. I forgot to ask if anyone else was in here. Lord, I hoped not! What I saw made me gasp.

I stepped all the way inside and was transported into a tropical rainforest paradise. I always considered myself to have an excellent imagination; it was nothing compared to the designers of this spa. Where I had been expecting flat tile floors and a large garden tub with jets, possibly sleek shiny tiles on the walls, I found smooth, round river rock with light tan grout. Elephant ears, bird of paradise, ferns, umbrella plants, jasmine, and hibiscus surrounded me. I even saw at least five palm trees. I couldn't name half of the plants and trees that enveloped this room if I tried.

The ceiling was painted a dusky blue, Tiki torch lanterns lit up a stepping stone path further into the room, not that it was truly dark in here. I could hear the surge of bubbling water but couldn't yet see it. Faintly in the background, there was even a soundtrack of rustling leaves, chirping insects, and the occasional bird songs. It was truly magnificent.

Padding barefoot down the stepping stone trail, I discovered the jacuzzi tucked just enough behind two of the palms to remain concealed until the last second. When I finally stumbled upon it, the designers had successfully created a jaw-dropping awe factor. I stood transfixed. My eyes raked up the side of the ashy black rock to the lip of the volcano in front of me where, raised about three feet off the ground, the bubbling water waited, steam curling from the top and rising slowly toward the ceiling.

Oh. My. Gosh. I was giddy with anticipation. I found the discreetly concealed steps and made my way to the jacuzzi. Empty! Looks like it was my lucky day. A relaxing soak, alone, in the tropical pool heated by a "volcano". Twenty minutes might not be enough.

Dipping my toes into the steamy water, I debated whether to get acclimated to the heat or just get in and get it over with. Finding it to be less than lobster-boiling temperature, thank goodness, I decided to climb in right away.

Resting my legs on the long bench seat, I sank lower down until my chin dipped the water with my head resting on the edge of the tub. Now this, this was the life. I wondered how Sam was enjoying the steam room. I also wondered what exactly a steam room would be like; it was going to be another first for me. Finally, I shut my thoughts down and just listened to the peaceful serenade of the forest; relished the feel of the jets massaging my back, neck. and feet.

Minutes passed. At some point later, I thought I heard the faint click of the door. "Sam?" I called out.

Nothing. Checking the small egg timer by my towel I saw there were still eight minutes left. *I must have been mistaken*, I decided. Shrugging my shoulders, I settled back into the water without giving another thought to the noise.

Sweat was rolling down my forehead by the time my jacuzzi session was over. "Whew!" I said to the steamy air. Carefully making my way down from the volcano pool, I took the time to dry off and was wrapping the towel around me when I heard the door open, for sure this time. The sound was followed by an immediate shriek that sent chills down my body, "Eeeeekkk!"

I took off down the path at lightning speed, swiping foliage out of my face.

"Sam, what…" I began but she cut me off waving and pointing on the stones between us.

"Snakes! Eeeee snaaaakessss!" Her squeal morphed into a cry.

Sure enough, two long, green snakes were coming right toward me on the path. Samantha was lucky she hadn't stepped on them coming in the door. They certainly weren't there when I came in.

"Piper, what do we do? I can't, I just can't! Oh yuck!" Sam was terrified of snakes, not to mention completely grossed out by them. She flattened herself against the door, standing on her toes trying to be as far from the slithery creatures as possible.

Lucky for us, I wasn't as frozen by them as she was. I also knew that most variations of the green snakes were non-poisonous, with the exception of the green mamba and I was seriously praying a green mamba hadn't found a way here from Africa. Armed with that knowledge, I yanked the nearest thing, a bird of paradise, out of its pot and tossed the dirt to the side. Cautiously, I stepped toward the snakes. Sam was squealing and jumping up and down, but my friend could have run out the door and left me; the fact that she didn't spoke volumes.

Slamming the pot down over the snakes, I let out a shaky breath. "Let's get out of here."

Just as we opened the door, Margarite and Jill were approaching. "Sorry we are late," Jill said.

"There was a commotion in the suite," Margarite added, wringing her hands together. I bet she had never been late in her life.

"What kind of commotion?" I crossed my arms.

"Gladys thought she heard someone, but there was nobody there," Jill explained.

Sam and I shot each other a look. Well, Gladys's presence might be accounted for, but was it a distraction to keep someone away from the jacuzzi room longer?

Sam, still fairly shaken up, pointed to the jacuzzi room and snapped. "Well, we had a little commotion of our own. Perhaps someone can explain to me just when snakes were added to the jacuzzi room? The new rainforest theme was great but I don't think it was necessary to add creatures as well."

Margarite's eyes grew round.

"Snakes?" Jill furrowed her brow. "What do you mean snakes?"

"Two of them," I told her. "Alive."

Margarite passed out in a heap on the floor.

"Oh!" Jill knelt, waving air toward Margarite's face.

"I'll get Broussard," Sam jogged down to the hallway, turning right at the wide corridor. She was back in moments with Broussard who lifted Margarite and carried her away. "I will send a temporary assistant," he added over his shoulder.

"You can just send them to my room," Sam told him. Turning to me, she apologized, "I'm sorry to bail but I just can't go in there wondering if there might be more of those…yuck… those snakes." She trembled just talking about it.

"It's fine. Hey, I can come with you back to the suite, no big deal," I assured her.

"No Piper. I would feel horrible. Please, go on in the steam room; I want you to experience everything while you're here."

"Fine," I reluctantly agreed, "but Jill is going to see that you make it to the room okay. No arguments."

Sam opened her mouth, presumably to protest, but Jill nodded at me and said, "Absolutely. Come now Miss Samantha, I'll happily walk back with you. Piper," she added to me, "I'll be back to collect you in twenty minutes. Your honey scrub should already be inside."

I watched until they disappeared down the hallway and then turned to the steam room. I'd been standing there in my bikini the whole time, evidently having lost my towel in the chaos with the snakes, so I pulled open the door handle and went right in.

The heat nearly knocked me over by the time I reached the bench across the room. I struggled to draw a breath, not expecting the thick, heavy steam to be quite so overpowering. I sank to the bench and felt the small porcelain bowl next to me. Figuring if I were going to do this, I might as well do it all, I smeared the cream up and down my legs. It was still cool in comparison to the hot steam so I applied it everywhere, from my forehead down my neck, behind my shoulders, over my chest and stomach. I was running low by the time I reached my arms.

The drops of sweat I shed in the jacuzzi were nothing; I was dripping water like a leaky faucet. My goodness, twenty minutes of this and I would lose eight pounds of water weight. I leaned my head back to minimize the sweat running in rivulets into my eyes. My breaths grew harsher and I realized I was really struggling to breathe. I sat up straight and became light-headed.

Just as I was about to give up and leave, I saw a silhouette on the other side of the glass door. Oh good, I thought, lying my head on my knees, Jill must be here to get me.

I stood, heading to the door but instead of someone opening it, I saw the figure disappear. Odd. Arriving at the door, I turned the handle. Nothing happened. I wiggled it but the door didn't budge. I sank to the floor, hot and weak; so thirsty.

I'm not sure how long I slumped in the floor; I'm certain it couldn't have been much longer when a scraping noise alerted me and then the door opened and I crawled out.

"Oh!" a startled Jill jumped backward. Then pulling herself together she helped me to my feet and steered me into a shower at the end of the hall. Turning on barely lukewarm water, she pushed me inside. It worked. The water cooled my skin and cleared the fog from my brain. I shut the stream of water off and inhaled blessed cool air, in and out, deeply over and over again.

"I'm so sorry, are you okay?" Jill asked.

"I am now," I told her as she handed me a towel to wrap around my bathing suit. "I couldn't get out," I said.

"Yes, I saw, it seems the coat rack fell off the wall and was blocking the door. I'll see to it that someone checks all of the others and tightens them up."

"Did you come by a few minutes ago and then leave?" I asked her.

"No, I just arrived and found the coat rack blocking the door."

"Someone else was there. I saw someone through the glass, I think they tried to lock me in."

"What? Are you certain it wasn't the heat?"

"I'm sure I saw someone."

"Let's get you into some dry clothes. I'm sure we will figure it out."

I allowed her to lead me down the myriad of hallways back to our suites. "I'll send someone for your clothes in the locker room," Jill promised. "Right now, I think you should lie down."

I could tell by her furtive glances that she was afraid I too might pass out at any moment. I was also fairly certain she didn't believe me, but I knew I saw someone at the door right before I tried opening it. Just like I was now thinking someone had put those snakes in the jacuzzi room when I heard the click of the door the first time.

Gladys was in the sitting room when we arrived, reading a book in the window seat. "Samantha went to have a nap," she told me. "My goodness," she yelped, "you're so pale. Are you okay?"

At that moment Sam's door opened and she came out yawning. "I thought I heard voices. How was the steam room, Piper?" she asked.

"I'm going to leave you here with your friends," Jill said. "Please consider resting before lunch."

"What happened? Oh my gosh, were there more snakes?" Sam asked as the door shut behind Jill.

"No. Someone locked me in the steam room, Sam." My stomach lurched. Saying it out loud made it worse. Who would do that?

"What?" she made me tell her the whole story. "You know, I think I will go lay down for a few minutes," I said when I was done. "Jill should be bringing my other clothes, or sending someone with them."

My eyes were already drooping, so I stripped off my wet clothes huddled into the covers and closed my eyes.

SEVEN

The nap helped, and I felt refreshed after ten or fifteen minutes. Sam came in to wake me, handing me a bag she said had been returned from the locker. I pulled my cargo pants back on that I had worn most of the morning, hoping lunch was more casual than dinner.

Sam, Gladys and I agreed that perhaps Jill was right and the heat made me think someone was in the hall by the steam room when really there was no one.

Since we could see a portion of the back garden from the windows in our suite, where late lunch should be currently, we rebelled against the personal assistant protocol and made the short trip outside on our own. Besides, Sam knew the way from being party to previous events held here by her mother.

Of all the menus in this place, still, none were of food. There were no menus to be found for lunch at least; instead, a buffet was set out on trestle tables with bright white table runners which were set up around the entire perimeter of the garden.

The garden itself was gorgeous. Palms, banana trees, enormous oleander, hibiscus – every conceivable tropical plant had been planted to maximum advantage resulting in a breathtaking paradise that was nestled at the side of the spa's dining room exit. I was relieved to see the buffet was filled with real food, not those horrid little hors d'oeuvres; tables nearly buckled under the weight of sandwiches, roasted chicken, several salad options, hummus, nuts, potato salad, even a chip and dip section.

Most importantly, there was a table devoted to desserts. Tarts, cookie bars, a dark chocolate fondue fountain, banana pudding, petit fours, bonbons. I may have whimpered aloud judging by the looks I was getting from my friends as well as the table of ladies near my elbow. Dessert was just what I needed to fully recover from my steam room ordeal.

Sam, Gladys, and I each snagged a square, plastic gold plate and loaded them down. Many of the round tables being used for seating were full, but we did find one at the edge of the garden near the path to the beach with only two women seated at it.

"Pardon. May we join you?" Sam asked as we approached.

One lady, an elderly woman with a shock of short white hair, inclined her head towards the empty chairs. "Why of course, please do."

"Thank you so much," I told them sincerely. I mean, I would have eaten sitting in the grass but at this fancy place, I assumed that type of behavior would get us removed.

"I'm Gladys, these young ladies are my friends, Samantha and Piper," Gladys took the chair closest to the white-haired lady.

"Please, you can call me Sam," Sam added with a smile.

Smiling in return, the older lady continued the introductions, "Pleasure to meet you three. I'm Eloise and this is my daughter Belle."

Belle, who looked to be maybe eighteen or nineteen years old, shyly waved her fingers at us before hiding her face behind a goblet of lemonade. Lemonade! "Excuse me," I asked, "where did you find lemonade? I didn't see the drinks and that looks like heaven."

"Oh! Well, they were behind the fountain, just there," Belle pointed across the garden to a large marble fountain of angels. I could just see corners of white tablecloth poking out from behind it.

"Great! Thanks, Belle. Gladys, what can I get you to drink?"

"A water will be fine, Piper."

"Wait, I'll come too," Sam folded her napkin and placed it neatly next to her plate. I looked at my wadded-up napkin in my chair smirking to myself; Sam would hate it if I told her that her mother's lady lessons were more evident than she realized.

There was a short line at the drink table so we fell in step to the slow-moving rhythm. My stomach grumbled. Maybe I should have brought some of those chips with me over here, I thought to myself glancing over my shoulder. As I did, I saw a figure disappear behind one of the many palms and leaned to see around it.

"What are you staring at? Your food isn't going anywhere now move, you're holding up the line," Sam chastised.

"I could have sworn I just saw someone familiar," I told her, "but I didn't catch a good look."

Sam glanced back but by now the figure was long gone.

"Who do you think you saw? There are probably twenty-five other people out here Piper."

"Never mind, you're right, it doesn't matter."

Throat clearing and whispers behind hands made it clear we were getting on the nerves of those in line behind us. Stepping quickly forward, I picked up two glasses of ice, placing one under the water and one under the lemonade jars and pushing the spigots for each.

Making our way back to the table, Sam greeted several people. Her mother's cousin Maisy, her old friend from grade school Rachael, and others who I didn't know.

"Are you sure you aren't campaigning to be the next mayor?" I teased as we drew near our chairs.

"Very funny, Piper." Sam glared.

Handing Gladys her water, I sat down and dug into the roast chicken on my plate. I was feeling absolutely famished and the chicken did not disappoint, moist, tender, and extremely well-seasoned with light barbecue spices. In fact, everything I ate was delicious, only serving to build my anticipation for the desserts. Finally, unable to stand it any longer, I pushed my plate with the last helpings of potato salad aside and pulled my dessert plate to me.

Now, what to try first? The rocky road brownie bite, vanilla bean sugar cookie, blueberry tart, or carrot cake petit four?

"Piper! Earth to Piper," Sam caught my attention.

"Yes," I looked up to see the entire table looking at me. Whoops, I guess I may be a little too into my dessert because it looked like I had tuned out everyone else.

"Gladys was just asking if she might taste your blueberry tart," Sam nodded over at Gladys who was smiling with a slight twinkle in her eye.

"Oh, er, yes. Of course," spinning the plate so the tart rested closer to Gladys, I expected her to cut off a bite. Imagine my surprise when the tart was scooped up and placed on her plate whole.

"Piper you're a doll," she said. "I love blueberries." Turning to Eloise she kept right on talking, thankfully missing the dropped-jaw look I was sporting.

Somewhat sarcastically I asked, "Would anyone else like anything?" And darn if Belle didn't look wistfully at my vanilla bean sugar cookie. Noting the severe lack of anything but salad on the plates she and her mother had eaten, I took pity on her. Sensing she was too shy to ask, I held the plate out to her, "Here Belle, why don't you try this cookie. Obviously, I have plenty of desserts, who needs three anyway."

Sam discreetly covered her laugh with a cough into her napkin. She knew I would gladly have eaten three whole plates just as easily as three tiny desserts.

Belle glanced at her mother, still busy discussing the good old days with Gladys, and quickly took the beautiful cookie which was covered in powdered sugar lace. "Thank you, Piper."

The carrot cake was perfect and the rocky road brownie had me seriously considering whether or not I could fit the whole platter in my purse to sneak back to my suite; unfortunately, I hadn't carried a purse to lunch so the point was moot. "Drat," I muttered.

"What?" Sam asked.

"Nothing."

With lunch over it was time to find the room for pedicures. Not surprisingly, our assistants were waiting for us right inside the doorway when we returned to the building from the garden.

"How was lunch?" Jill asked.

"Fantastic," I rubbed my belly.

Lola motioned us to hurry, "We are nearly late," she whispered. "I think Margarite would faint if her charge were late anywhere."

Picking up our pace, the three of us followed along down several more hallways in a new direction. "I'm pretty sure I could get lost in this place," I told Gladys and Sam.

I slipped my hands into my pockets as we walked and felt the crumpled-up paper from earlier. Pulling it out, I opened it and stopped walking, staring at it in disbelief. Similar to the note at the bakery, it was capitalized to read: **I TOLD YOU - YOU CAN'T HAVE EVERYTHING**.

Sam noticed me lagging behind and slowed down. I caught up to her and silently handed over the note. After a sharp intake of breath, she whispered, "Where did this come from?"

"Do you remember when my slippers went missing?"

At her nod I continued, "Evidently someone left this in their place. I thought it was garbage. I don't know what made me open it just now."

"Taking your slippers though, really?"

"Yep. I would say someone either doesn't like me or is playing a really elaborate prank."

"But who?"

"That's what I can't figure out. There was nobody but us and the employees in the room for the foot massage. I haven't seen any of them before at the bakery."

"And Gladys."

"What?" I asked.

Sam shrugged. "Gladys. She's been at the bakery and here with us at the spa."

Before I could tell her what a crazy theory I thought that sounded like, Gladys herself called over her shoulder, "Come on slowpokes. I'm going to pick hideous colors for your toes if you don't hurry it up."

I raised my eyebrow at Sam, "No, surely not," I whispered.

We hurried to catch up before the group rounded the corner at the end of the hallway. I hated to think it. It didn't seem possible, but I was going to keep an eye on Gladys.

Arriving at the salon wing, Margarite led us past the hairstylists' rooms and waxing rooms to a long row of chairs at the back. These weren't just any chairs, of course. They were top of the line, deluxe leather armchairs that reclined. At the foot of the chair, instead of a footrest popping out, there was a large basin of water attached to the chair.

"Oh my gosh!" I said settling into the chair Jill led me to.

"What? What is it?" Sam said, eyes wide. The note had obviously set her on edge.

Not taking my eyes from it, I held up the object of my surprise. "It has almost thirty massage settings!"

Sam closed her eyes and I could almost visually see the numbers rolling behind her eyelids as she silently counted to ten and blew out a deep breath. "That's it," she said calmly, "you have to get out more. In fact, I tried to bring you for pedicures to the salon downtown millions of times, but you wouldn't come."

"Well excuse me but someone never mentioned a deluxe massage. I pictured lots of snipping and prodding at my toes and those horrible callus scrubs you always hear about with the cheese grater," I harrumphed. Secretly, I agreed with Sam. Obviously, I had been missing out on the small pleasures. Oh well, now I knew.

One of the nail technicians, a young girl with her hair in a short pixie cut and rings of dark eyeliner, wheeled a cart of polishes between me and Gladys.

"Welcome to O Heavenly Day Spa's Cloudless Day Salon. Care to pick a color?"

Sam, too far away from the cart to see, leaned over and nudged me. "Grab me something to match my hair please."

Examining the cart, I picked a gorgeous red and passed it to her. "How is this?"

She flipped the polish over and read the bottom aloud, "Abiding Love. I like it."

I think somewhere along the way I knew that nail polishes had names instead of regular colors, but I had forgotten. I decided it would be more fun to pick a color first before reading the name on any of the others.

I fingered a few turquoises, one or two pinks; I didn't want to choose red and match Sam's polish, so I steered clear of those.

Thoughts about Sam and her concerns that Gladys had the opportunity to place both of the disconcerting notes were still processing in the back of my mind. Glancing at Gladys, curious about her choice, I was shocked to see a glossy black polish in her hand. Black, really? Was she trying to match the tech's eyeliner?

"What color is that Gladys?" I asked her.

She waved the polish towards me. "You'll have to read it, Piper, I can't see this tiny writing."

Eyes widening, I read the name to her, "Lucifer." Beside me, I swear Sam gulped.

Okay. It is just a silly nail polish, I told myself. Now I just need to find myself a color and relax. Following Sam's lead, I chose a silver to match my hair and turned it over to peek at the name. Talk about weird coincidences; Angel's Hair, it was called.

"We're ready," Sam smiled sweetly at the desk manager; he pushed a button and as the girl wheeled the cart away three lean, short-haired men of Asian appearance came out and took their place on small, wheeled stools in front of us. I reclined my chair, but only slightly this time; I wanted to stay awake and aware. Gladys reclined her chair back as far as it would go. Sam stayed sitting straight up and mouthed "Lucifer??" at me with one raised eyebrow.

I shrugged. The jets in the footbath were fired up. They weren't quite as relaxing as the actual foot massage this morning, but the hot water felt nice. I chose a lavender and green tea sugar scrub from the menu to finish off my pedicure. This place and all their non-food menus threw me for a loop. Never in my life had I seen a place with so many choices.

Sam's sugar scrub was passionflower. Gladys chose mint. I had a fleeting thought that if Eloise were here, she would probably choose earl grey. Her poise and manners and superior demeanor towards her daughter all gave me a rather English impression.

My wandering mind was drawn back to the present when, at last, the nail tech in front of my chair picked up my foot and began trimming my toenails. He also removed all of the dead skin around the nail edges. Too soon it was time for the dreaded cheese grater tool, the callus sanding pedicure tool of doom. Turns out, I am ticklish on my feet. A lot.

Once I made it past the calluses being scrubbed ruthlessly from my heels, I really began to enjoy the pedicure. It was a foot massage all over again! After a deep kneading of both feet, the young guy at my station got up and walked toward cabinets at the side of the room.

"Psssst," I whispered.

Sam was reading the latest Food Network magazine next to me and paid no attention.

"Psst, Sam," I whispered again.

"What Piper?" she asked smirking.

"He didn't paint my toes. I thought they were supposed to paint your toes?"

"Ha!" Sam burst out laughing. Maybe I should start charging per laugh, one would think I was her own personal comedian these days. "Piper, you are nowhere near done with this pedicure. Zeng's just going to get the hot towels. Don't worry, the paint will get on your toenails before we leave." Apparently, Sam knew all of the staff.

I stuck my tongue out at her. Childish, maybe, but I like to think of it as cathartic. She grinned at me and turned back to her glossy magazine.

Sure enough, Zeng was back within two minutes bearing a silver tray of steaming pink towels. Unfolding the first one, he shook it out a few times and held it up to cool just a bit before tightly wrapping it from my knee to my ankle. Man! Whoever coined the phrase 'as fun as a wet blanket' must never have been introduced to these wonderful wet towels. With both legs wrapped in hot steamy cloth, I could feel my entire body heat.

"Woo, is it hot in here?" I fanned myself.

Like ordering up a miracle, the girl who wheeled around the polishes earlier suddenly appeared at my elbow.

"Orange water ma'am?" she offered me a cold glass of ice water with three thin orange slices swimming happily in it.

"Thank you, yes." I sipped it slowly. The cold and the citrus were refreshing and I gulped the rest of the glass down.

"I'll have one of those please," Sam said.

Gladys declined, "If you happen to have cucumber water, I would love one of those though."

The girl went to a fridge concealed behind the counter and returned with icy cucumber water in a short glass.

Sam's toes were nearly finished I noticed. The older gentleman was finishing up her last two toes in red.

Zeng unwrapped the now much cooler towels from my legs and smoothed lotion all over them, massaging my calf as he went. If I hadn't seen Sam and Gladys receive the same treatment, I would have been uncomfortable. I laughed at myself inwardly, before this trip was over people were going to be rubbing all over my body so my leg should be fine. My face heated as I recalled the accidental phone call with Griff, discussing my massage wardrobe.

"Look at my sexy toes!" Gladys stretched her feet out for us to see, nearly kicking the poor guy still in front of her.

I frowned, "Gladys, I don't think you can say sexy at a church."

"We aren't at a church, we are at a spa."

"Besides," Sam joined in, "you just said sexy too."

I rolled my eyes, "We are so getting kicked out before four days are over."

EIGHT

I have to admit that Gladys's nails do look incredible. Instead of painting the whole nail, she had the manicurist do French tips with the black, giving them a more elegant look.

I was perfectly happy with mine as well. The silver had a tiny metallic sparkle to it so they seemed to sparkle in the light.

Sam's red toes were gorgeous; we all agreed when we returned to the suites that sandals to showcase our feet were a must for dinner.

I was doubly glad I had picked Angel's Hair silver for my color as I considered what to wear for dinner. At least my nails would match basically anything. Upon returning to our suites, I entered my set of rooms and was more than pleased with the theme. To be quite honest, I hadn't even spared it a glance when I went in for the first time to nap after my troubling trip to the steam room. Now, however, I spun in a slow circle and gave it my full attention.

The fluffy, cloud-painted ceiling continued in my suite, but the remainder of the décor was in soft, muted tones. The walls were a light, sandy linen color. A couple of bamboo plants decorated the room, including one corner where bamboo was erected on two sides, with a wall on the third, to create a changing screen. The carpet was a luscious green.

I found my suitcase unpacked, stowed in the corner. All of my dresses, a whopping three, were hung in the massive walk-in closet. Jill, or someone, had even hung up my t-shirts. How many days did people usually stay here to need all of that space?

My extra set of cargo pants, yoga pants, and my sleep shorts were all folded neatly in the dresser drawers (also in the closet, it was that big!). I shook my head. This place was nothing if not efficient.

My purse sat on the divan at the foot of the bed. Sam and I had agreed to shut down our phones for this trip, but I thought I had better check in just in case. Powering the phone up I was relieved, and not wholly surprised, to find no missed calls or messages. After checking the time, four-thirty in the afternoon, I turned it off and headed to take a long, hot shower. The en-suite master bath was a bonus I hadn't expected. I may not be a primp-and-preen girl, but if I were going to get dressed up for dinner, it was going to take some work.

A knock sounded at my door just after I finished blow-drying my hair. When I opened it, Gladys stood at the door to my suite holding two dresses. "Piper, which do you think?" she asked.

I looked at the options. Seriously, was I the only person without the appropriate attire? One was a simple black dress, fluted shoulders, round neck, and belted with a bright red scarf. The other was sparkly gold sequins, lower cut but with golden fishnet that came up into a high collar at the neck.

"Wow. They are both beautiful," I told her honestly.

"What are you wearing?" she asked peering around me.

"I don't know," I shrugged.

"Oh," Gladys's shoulders drooped and I gave in.

"Wear the black one, save the gold for our last night here," I winked and closed the door. Great, now what was I going to wear?

I made my way to the walk-in closet and flipped on the light switch. I pulled the three dresses from the bar and hung them from the top drawer of the dresser, looking at them side by side. I had a short blue sundress with yellow daisies, a black and turquoise sleeveless A-line dress, and a white, off the shoulder, shift dress that reached just above my knees. None were even half as elegant as Gladys's two choices and I couldn't imagine what Sam would be wearing. Not that I cared, I reminded myself. These will do just fine. I pulled the black and turquoise dress off the hanger and left the others staring silently after me.

The dress didn't look bad at all. It was simple but the turquoise complimented my hair and the black made it formal enough I supposed. My thoughts were interrupted by more knocking, though this time though the door opened and Sam came right in without waiting on me to answer it.

"Hey," she smiled. "You look great Piper. Can you zip me?"

"Thanks. Of course," I motioned for her to spin and she held her hair while I zipped up her selection for the night. Black bodice with empire waist, lace cutout in the back making the zipper a very delicate thing by her shoulder blades, and a short black and red chevron pattern for the skirt.

"I don't remember this dress," I told her. "It looks amazing on you."

"I bought it a few weeks ago, you know, back when my hair was pink? Well, obviously it clashed too badly to wear it then so tonight is its debut."

"Good choice," I commended her, mostly for choosing not to wear red with pink hair because I could only imagine how painful to the eye that would be; though, probably not on Sam since she looked beautiful in everything she put on. I think it was her confidence that did it, not even the clothes.

"I'll be out in a minute," I told Sam. "Just let me finish my hair."

After braiding the top half of my hair and adding eyeliner and mascara to my eyes, I turned off the bathroom light and slipped on some small black heels.

Sam and Gladys were waiting in the sitting room; Sam clapped her hands when I joined them, her enthusiasm making her long curls bounce. "Oh great, we all match," she grinned.

~

I should have known there was some reason for Sam to be glad we matched. Walking over to the dining hall, which was in a separate building along with the kitchen, just to the side of the garden, Sam said, "Piper, by the way, we have an interview with Pastor Dan and his assistant for the church newsletter over dinner this evening."

"Why?" I asked.

"They would like to thank us for all of the fundraisings that we did and give the Ooey-Gooey-Goodness Bakery a little spotlight feature in return. I'm sure they will want to know more about your friend Landon so they can bring more awareness to the very real danger of human trafficking, even in the United States."

"Okay," I steeled myself. "If it possibly helps anyone else avoid or escape from the hell that Landon went through, then it will be worth it. It feels kind of odd though since it isn't really my story to tell."

The dining hall wasn't nearly as opulent as the spa itself. Dark and rustic, the long wooden tables that filled the room ensured that diners sat close enough together for fellowship and encouraged inclusion rather than leaving some to sit alone at a corner table. The floor was a beautiful reddish brown twelve-inch tile pattern. The ceilings were standard eight feet drop height with plenty of lights illuminating everything.

On the tables were - be still my heart - menus! Yes, I am excited to see a menu that doesn't involve a foot scrub or a toenail clipping. Not that lunch wasn't scrumptious, but I was still eager to see what a formal dinner menu here was comprised of when everything else was so fancy.

The menu did not disappoint. Rack of lamb. Filet Mignon. Baked Alaskan Salmon. Parmesan Herb Chicken. Smothered Pork Chops. Grilled Asparagus. Veggie skewers. Garlic potatoes. Salads whose ingredients looked more complex than my cookie recipes. Soup. And not a snail in sight, thank goodness.

We were seated towards the head of one row of long tables. A young woman appeared to take our orders: Baked Salmon for Gladys, Parmesan Herb Chicken for Sam, and I chose the Filet Mignon. The room was only half full, so the noise level was still fairly quiet. We chatted about inconsequential things and before long Sam waved to Pastor Dan. He and a middle-aged woman in a muted gray pantsuit made their way to our table.

Pastor Dan pulled out a chair for his assistant as he introduced her to us, "This is Winnie," he told us. "She is in charge of our newsletter and will be taking notes this evening. But we can get to business later. First, how are you ladies enjoying your stay?" he smiled widely.

Sam and I glanced at each other; the pastor didn't seem aware of the mishaps that went on today.

Gladys broke the silence. "Well," she started in a huff.

I cut her off, "It has been wonderful. Thank you." Might as well not hash through the whole day again. I figured it wasn't the pastor's fault snakes got into the spa, after all..

"Excellent, happy to hear it!" If he smiled any wider, I was afraid his face might break. The waitress stopped by to get the newcomers' orders. The more we chatted the more I realized Pastor Dan was just a genuinely happy and jovial man. He had plenty of laughs over antics of Sam as a child. He asked about Griffin as well.

Finally, after we had all scraped our plates clean of the divine food, Winnie asked if we would mind beginning the interview. They had succeeded in putting me completely at ease and I was happy to begin.

"Do you mind if we discuss it over dessert?" I asked. "There was a triple chocolate decadent cake, layered with mousse, that I would love to try."

"I'll share it with you," Sam agreed. The others ordered coffee, declaring themselves simply too stuffed to indulge in another thing for the evening.

Dessert was brought to the table. It was out of this world in flavors and the mousse might have been fluffier than the pillows on my bed. And so, we began the interview.

"We want to thank you very much for all the money your bakery raised for Breaking Chains. A little birdy told me you donated fifty percent of your profits to this cause the last few weeks?"

My cheeks warmed with embarrassment.

"Yes, sir." Sam said, "Piper and I agreed it would be wonderful to win, but we didn't really expect to since ours is a fairly new business compared to those who have been established here for generations. However, more than that, we agreed that every bit we could afford to give to this mission was more than worth it."

"We decided to think big," I added. "We brainstormed ways to draw in more customers; anything from the dessert of the week samples to calling in at the city and offering a ten percent discount to allow us to cater events; we even set up snack stands at some of the beach volleyball games. When we saw it was working, more business was flowing in, we also made signs and put a donation box in the bakery itself."

"That's right," Sam picked up. "And people were more than generous. We took down the tip jar and asked them to give solely to the fundraiser. We couldn't have raised the money without so many extraordinary, generous members of our community."

Winnie nodded after she finished writing and asked, "Piper, did Sam know about your friend Landon when you both agreed to raise money for Breaking Chains?"

I shook my head, "No. I have never really talked about it. And that is the real problem. Nobody talks about it when things like that happen. Nobody wants to admit it is possible because that's scary. And nobody wants to admit it happens even where they live because that is embarrassing and would require someone to take responsibility for it."

I sipped my unsweet tea before continuing. "I thought the fundraiser would be enough. That it would make me feel good for helping. And it did, but not completely. That was when I realized I needed to talk about it. Not to feel better, or unburden me, but to encourage others to talk about it too. To make it real and not allow it to be another opportunity to toss money at something and move on."

"Can you tell us more about how your friend Landon was successfully recovered? Were police looking for him?"

"I didn't understand a lot of this until I got older. The information is out there, but only if you are looking for it in most cases. To answer your questions, the police had given up the search for Landon months earlier. The body of one of the girls abducted with him was found in a dumpster. She had obviously been raped; her death was from a head injury. My parents told me this when I was a teenager."

"Oh Piper," Sam placed a supportive hand on my shoulder.

"The police got a tip about a house with 'lots of young punks' coming in and out. The caller also said the windows were boarded over and that a van frequently backed into the carport, up to the door, and nothing that was unloaded could be seen. Trash bags were taped inside the door windows so that you couldn't see in from the street. These are often a few of the signs of houses with drugs or prostitution rings being run out of them so the police sent a team to check it out."

"Really?" Winnie seemed quite blown away by all the information. She appeared to realize she had forgotten to take notes and furiously scribbled into her notebook giving me a few moments of reprieve. Sam and I ate a few more bites of the chocolate cake while we waited for Winnie's pen to take another break.

"Of course, sometimes a boarded-up window is just that – a broken window someone couldn't afford to replace. There are so many things that make human trafficking hard for law enforcement to pinpoint, or sometimes even identify as the real crime in a given situation."

"Can you explain what you mean?" Pastor Dan asked, tilting his head to the side in a quizzical manner.

"I can try. Take prostitution, for example, obviously, commercial sex is a crime. So often though, teens engaged in commercial sex were either forced, threatened or manipulated in a way that they never found any other choice. A pimp may find a runaway on the street and offer food and protection in exchange for services, or they might dose a kidnapped boy or girl with drugs consistently to get them addicted and when their body screams out in withdrawal the pimp offers a solution: sex with some new people for a fix. There are so many times that the person caught is a victim, but receives full punishment, while the traffickers and controllers themselves just replace them with fresh inventory and keep operating business as usual."

My emotions were getting stirred up, I took a sip of my tea to cool down. "Landon and children like him don't want to do bad things. Unfortunately, most of them also don't know how to get home, they can't work to provide food for themselves if they did escape, and often the fear of beatings or starvation keep them in line doing whatever they are asked to do in order to survive. Landon was blessed to be rescued. Many aren't."

"I'm sorry to ask this, but what about individuals rescued from that type of situation who, years later, are found to be right back in it? Are you saying they are still victims?" Winnie asked, but she seemed genuinely trying to sort through it, not judgmental or sarcastic.

"Once you have been in that life for a long time, I think it would be hard to fight through the fear, the shame, the guilt and the worthlessness that was pressed upon you, so yes, some may embrace it as they get older. They embrace it to numb themselves, an emotional survival decision is just as real as physical survival." I sighed, emotionally exhausted, "I don't know how to help people like that, just like I had no idea how to help my childhood friend who had been exposed to situations I couldn't even imagine. That is why it is so important to support organizations like Breaking Chains who are better prepared to provide the counseling and services for many aspects of human trafficking victims, and why it is important to raise awareness and open our hearts to understanding. A lot more goes on than the caption our mind writes for the picture we think we see."

Pastor Dan placed his hands over mine, "Piper, thank you for sharing. And Sam, thank you both for what your business did to join with us in this mission. Each of the businesses that participated has made a huge impact for Breaking Chains and I can only guess at how far God will use those proceeds to provide help for the men, women, and children entrapped in this modern-day slavery."

I pushed the last few bites of cake away, my thoughts too heavy to eat any more.

NINE

I awoke the next day feeling renewed after an extra-long night's sleep; Sam, Gladys and I had agreed to turn in early after such a long and eventful first day.

Lying in bed wondering whether or not Sam or Gladys would be awake yet, I was surprised to hear a muffled knock on the sitting room door. I slipped my robe on over my Wonder Woman pajamas and opened the door to my suite. Gladys was ushering in Lola, the bearer of a silver tray laden with mouth-watering goodies.

"Room service," Gladys swept her hand toward the coffee table as Lola set everything out including glasses of orange juice and water.

Sam's door swung open. "Do I smell bacon?"

"Not if I get to it first," I joked.

"Don't you dare," she shrieked, sprinting across the room. "I'll send Griff pictures of you in those pajamas if you don't hand over the bacon."

I dropped the bacon back onto the platter as if it burnt me. Sam snickered and I mentally kicked myself, why did I care what Griff thought of my sleepwear anyway.

"You two are such a hoot," Gladys gave a barking laugh. "Makes me wish Harold and I had children of our own."

Sam tossed me half a piece of bacon, smirking. We enjoyed a leisurely breakfast and chatted about what we should choose for our spa treatments today.

"I think we should do a little less today," I told them. "That much relaxing nearly wore me out!"

Sam rolled her eyes, but I know my best friend loves me so I just threw toast at her and let it go.

"Thanks for ordering breakfast by the way Gladys," Sam said.

"Yes, definitely. Sam, we may have to think about adding these walnut and honey donuts to our menu. Maybe we can turn them into Walnut and Honey Donut Hole Clusters?"

"Mmmmhmmm," Gladys mumbled around a mouthful.

"Okay, so doing less today. We had five total treatments yesterday. What do you two say to four today – two in the morning and two after lunch?" Sam asked.

"Perfect," I told her.

"I'm happy with that," Gladys agreed easily, "in fact there is only one I'm curious about and you girls can pick the other three."

"Which do you want to do?" I asked Gladys as I snagged several menus and propped my feet on the arm of my chair.

"The seaweed wraps."

I choked on a forkful of scrambled eggs. "I'm sorry, the what?" Surely, she was joking. Right. Please let her be joking. What do they wrap in seaweed anyway?

"The seaweed wraps," Gladys repeated. "I've never heard of one before and I want to try it."

"What the heck do they wrap in seaweed?" I asked out loud.

"Oh boy," Sam rolled her head backward and stared at the ceiling. I bet she was counting again. Sitting back up she rolled her shoulders, "Okay so a seaweed wrap it is. Piper, any requests?"

"Yes, actually," I skimmed down the list. "What about Yoga for Flexibility? We've always talked about taking a yoga class but never have."

"Seaweed wraps and yoga, it is. Followed by lunch and a deep tissue massage then on to bejeweled nails."

"We just did our toes yesterday," I pointed out.

"Today we will do fingers!" Sam clapped her already manicured nails. How she keeps them so nice working in the bakery I have no idea.

"What is bejeweled?" Gladys asked. Finally, something I wasn't the only person out of the know on.

"Bejeweled means they will glue little fake jewels and colored pieces onto our nails. You can make designs or just have one on each nail – whatever you want really." Sam explained.

"Since we've decided, I guess I can ring Jill to place our order and get a schedule approved for today." Swinging my legs off of the chair, I slid my feet into the cozy slippers and went to the intercom, which thankfully this time didn't go off right as I got to it. Pushing the button, I spoke clearly, "Jill, this is Piper."

"Yes, Piper, I know," her light laughter fizzled in through the intercom.

"Oh. Okay. Well, we're ready to order. Our treatments. We are ready to order our spa treatments. We already ordered breakfast." I leaned my head against the wall while Sam fell onto the floor laughing.

"I'll be right there," Jill spoke sounding suspiciously like she was snorting back laughter of her own.

"Look," I glared at Sam, "it is just too weird ordering people around through a button."

"Why?" she asked wide-eyed. "You do it all the time when you go through the Baskin Robbin's drive-thru." I snatched up the throw pillow nearest the fireplace and tossed it at her head.

Jill rapped quickly on the door and entered without waiting for an answer. "Lola is on the way, but I'm afraid Margarite has been given the rest of the week off Samantha. Broussard is in a fit trying to find you 'a personal assistant suitable to your personal self' though, so I'm sure you will have someone soon." Her stuffy and straight-faced impersonation of Broussard had us each cracking up until Lola came in through the cracked door.

"What in the world did you all have for breakfast," she asked, "because I want some."

~

We polished off the breakfast tray while Jill and Lola took care of scheduling our appointments for the day. After they had returned and given us the official greenlight for our treatments - 9 AM Seaweed Wrap, 11 AM Yoga, 1 PM Lunch, 3:30 PM Deep Tissue Massage, and 5:00 PM Bejeweled Nail Session – we separated to our suites to dress, or undress basically, for the first one.

"Wear something skimpy," Sam tossed out over her shoulder as she entered her suite. "The seaweed wrap is full body." She shut the door with a giggle while I stood, mouth gaping, trying to wrap my mind around the thought of seaweed wrapping my body. All I could picture was feeling like a sushi roll, which was not my idea of a good time. If I'm being honest, sushi isn't even my idea of real food.

Gladys was ecstatic, "Oh I wonder if some handsome boy will be wrapping us!"

Bang, another door shut and I'm still standing here gaping like a fish. Seaweed was definitely not one of the things I planned to wear while I'd been on my accidental rant with Griff. And why was that even crossing my mind now. With a sinking feeling that this is going to shape up into another long day, I spin on my heel and march to my own suite.

Just as suspected, the bikini I wore yesterday, which happens to be both my only and skimpiest article of clothing suitable for being wrapped in seaweed, is still damp from yesterday's activities. I could borrow one of Sam's since we are similar in size, but honestly, I worry about what exactly she would lend me. Damp and uncomfortable it is. So, having tugged and pulled the wet fabric into place I throw on my robe and slippers, check my phone and toss it onto the bed, then return to the sitting room to read a few more food magazines while I wait for the others to be ready.

At eight forty-five Jill, Lola, and a particularly Broussard-like woman – no really, she even looked down her nose at me and sniffed in a similar fashion – appeared to "collect" us. The more they said it, the more I wanted to ask if they planned to stuff us and put us on a shelf.

"Miss Lowe," the new woman curtsied. She straight up curtsied! "I will be your temporary assistant until my brother is able to find someone of quality to be of service. I am Cynthia"

Ah, that explained it. She was Broussard's sister. I silently congratulated myself on catching the family resemblance so quickly, while at the same time wondering where the spa dug these people up. Surely, they would have been more at home butler-ing in a castle or something for "worthwhile" people in England than here in Seashell Bay where Americans were not respectful enough to keep the classes separate as obviously preferred by these two.

"Thank you. I assure you I don't require that much assistance actually." Sam's voice broke into my thoughts as she continued, "Please, tell your brother not to trouble himself on my behalf."

"It is on behalf of your mother, of course. We can't afford to lose our jobs," Sam tried to protest but Cynthia kept right on talking. "So, if you please, come with me. I need to escort you to your seaweed wrap so that you will not miss a moment of it."

Sam belted her robe, shrugged to me and Gladys and trailed behind Cynthia.

"Wow," I said to the room at large.

"Yes," Jill agreed. "Now are you ladies ready as well?"

Nodding, we made our way past the changing rooms and turned left down the hallway opposite of the nail salon. There we entered the room specifically set aside for seaweed wraps; I had noticed it yesterday but hadn't expected to subject myself to one. Still, here we were.

The inside of the room was painted in dark blues, grays, and greens. Dim lighting glowed from eight small can lights in the ceiling. One whole wall was an undersea kelp garden mural, beautifully depicted in vivid detail. The stalks fluidly bent as water weaved around them in the shadowy depths of the sea. It almost seemed to sway with the current. If you looked closely, just a few small fish had been added, darting in between the plants. I imagined they were playing a game of tag.

My admiration of the mural was interrupted when Jan, the aesthetician from yesterday's facial treatment incident, stepped between me and the mural. "Good morning ladies," she greeted us. Thankfully, her nose looked fine, not even a bandage. I was happy I hadn't actually hurt her.

"Morning Jan," Sam said. "These ladies have never had a seaweed wrap before," she murmured with a wink.

"Wonderful! You are going to love it," Jan told us. "Today the rest of the staff is back as well. This is Chloe and Rose."

I noticed Jan stayed on the opposite side of the room from me. Chloe was appointed to me. Each of the ladies pulled a large bowl off of the cabinet behind them. Goo, always more goo at this place.

Gladys must have been thinking the same thing, "Where's all the seaweed?" she asked crinkling her nose at the mixture Rose was bringing closer to her.

Jan snorted, actually snorted. "We don't actually wrap you in whole seaweed. Can you imagine, it would be falling off all over the place!"

Chloe took over the explanation, raising up the bowl she carried. "The seaweed is turned to a paste so that it maintains its rich array of sea salt, vitamins, iodine, and potassium. This paste is applied to your whole body."

"Then," Sam said, "they wrap us in towels and we lay in the dry sauna."

"This way," I whipped my head back to Jan who picked up the conversation, "your body is able to quickly and efficiently sweat out the impurities that the seaweed helps draw to the surface as the seaweed also loosens up dead skin cells."

"When you are all done," said Chloe, "you will shower off and come back here for a moisturizer to finalize your treatment."

"Don't forget the juice," Rose piped up for the first time, in a quiet voice.

"Ah yes," Jan smiled. "While in the sauna it can get quite hot, of course, and we do not need any of you dehydrating. Rose will make a mixture of juice and seaweed extract for you to drink, thus preventing dehydration and promoting detoxification from the inside out as well."

Giving an involuntary shudder, I glanced at Gladys.

"Are you happy?" I asked her. "We have to drink seaweed."

She mumbled something under her breath. Sam grinned at us both. I was starting to rethink my plans to visit this place with her in the future; I was right, pampering was overrated.

"I take it back," I said out loud half an hour later, covered in sludge. We were lying on bunk-bed type racks but with only wooden slats only, no cushion. The dry sauna was a dark room, the only illumination was the glow of the coals in the metal box heating the entire area and a few wispy beams of light sneaking through slats in the door.

"You take what back?" Sam asked from below me, in the middle bunk, over the sound of Gladys snoring on the bottom bunk.

"I take back all of the bad thoughts I was having about this place. This is my favorite room. So warm and toasty, do you think the landlord would let me put one of those coal boxes in my apartment?"

Gladys woke with a start, banging her head on the bunk in the process.

"Woo-wee," she exclaimed. "I think I'm going to have to get out of this inferno, it is just too hot in here for me."

I leaned over the wooden sides of my bunk to check on her.

"Did you hit your head? Will you be okay? Can you find your way back to Jan in the seaweed room?"

"Yes, yes," Gladys nodded, rubbing the back of one hand to her forehead while hitching up her towel with the other. "Stop fussing over me, I'm just a bit overheated is all. And no offense to the lovely spa, but I certainly don't think that nasty seaweed juice is going to be on the menu in heaven."

Laughing, I get comfortable on my bunk and silently agree with her; I had barely been able to drink my whole glass, and only because I didn't relish the idea of dehydration.

"Sam," I spoke quietly into the silence a few minutes later. "Do you think we will stay busy at the bakery, or do you think traffic will die back down now that we've been closed this whole weekend? What if people forget about Ooey-Gooey-Goodness?"

"I think it will be fine, Piper," she told me confidently.

"Well, how do you…" I started but stopped when Sam tapped my bunk and shushed me.

"Shh," Sam said, "do you hear that?"

An odd rustling noise made me turn my head and scan the room, but it was too dark to see anything.

The noise sounded again, like a small scratching, from much lower than my bunk. I rolled to the side, struggling to keep my towel secure. I really don't think we were supposed to be moving around this much in here, the wood was very unforgiving to hips and elbows.

"You don't think there are mice, do you?" Sam's voice quivered slightly.

I hoped not, or more snakes either, but I kept the thoughts to myself.

"No. Do you see anything?"

Just then, I saw a piece of paper slide out of one of the slats in the door. Right into the coal box. Whoosh! Flames munched at the corner of the paper. I jumped off my bunk, wincing as pain from the tile floor slammed into my bare feet, and swatted the paper out of the box. Sam scrambled out of her bunk and stomped the last embers out.

She looked at me and we both breathed a shaky smile of relief.

"Well, that was close," she said.

"Too close. The last thing we need in this room full of wood is a live fire."

"Do you think someone was trying to catch it on fire? Or that it just accidentally landed in the box of coals?"

"Only one way to find out," I nodded toward the paper, wisps of smoke rising from its corners, as I sank down onto the bottom bunk.

Sam grabbed the paper and sat beside me, unfolding it slowly.

YOU DON'T BELONG HERE

TEN

"We really have to sort out who is behind these notes," Sam sighed.

"I agree, plus I'm starting to think that the snakes and steam room incident might be related after all."

A quick rap at the door made us jump. I grabbed the note from Sam and stuffed it in the top of my towel.

"Miss Lowe, Miss Rivers," a voice came from the hall before the door swung open. Cynthia stood erect, hands clasped in front of her, while Jill hovered behind. "We are here to escort you to the showers and changing room if you please," Cynthia said as she narrowed her eyes. Obviously, we were supposed to be lying sedately in our bunks while we roasted, not engaging in friendly chit-chat.

"Of course," Sam smiled broadly, rising to her feet. "A shower would be lovely."

~

By the time we had showered, more people were in the changing rooms, so Sam and I postponed our discussion of the mysterious notes. Gladys was there as well, sitting on a bench and rubbing lotion into her hands and arms.

"Well, did you girls enjoy the rest of your time in the sauna?" she asked cheerfully.

She either had no idea about the near fire, which made sense because we hadn't told anyone, or she was pretending she didn't know about the note but was really behind them all. I hated that this new suspicion of everyone was beginning to creep into my thoughts.

"Yes, it was very enlightening, wouldn't you say, Piper?" Sam responded.

"Hmm, yes," I murmured agreement.

Jill came into the changing rooms and passed out what she called "yoga socks" to each of us. "Since you are going to group yoga next, I thought you might like to have some of these."

With non-slip grips on the bottom and separate places for all of your toes to go, it was like being barefoot except your feet didn't have to touch the yoga mats that tons of other people stood on barefoot.

"Thanks, Jill!" I told her. I hated going barefoot. My feet got cold quickly, so I was very happy about the socks.

"Look, Piper," Sam laughed, "I think everyone here is bound and determined to make sure nobody can tell my mother I walked around the spa barefoot." She wiggled her toes in the soft pink toe-socks.

Gladys, on the other hand, was struggling; it appeared she had at least three toes where the big toe should go. Shaking my head, I donned my own socks and let Jill lead me to the yoga and meditation studio. It was a large open space, sleek laminate wood flooring stretched from wall to wall making it look larger, and one wall housed a huge, probably ten feet by ten feet if I were to guess, picture window with a gorgeous view of the manicured lawn. The wall opposite of the door was a full, floor-to-ceiling mirror.

A few ceiling fans hummed slowly, and four other people milled about the room when Jill gestured me inside. I recognized one of them from our morning crowd at the bakery.

"Hi!" I greeted when she finished stretching.

"Oh, hi," she said as she tightened the elastic ponytail holder in her hair. "You're from the bakery, right? Piper?"

"That's me. And you are…" I thought a moment, "Barb? Barbara?"

"That's right, call me Barb," her smile brightened at being remembered. Points to me for customer service and name retention; Sam would be truly impressed because I'm terrible with names.

"Are you staying at the spa, too?" I asked. Barb appeared to be in her late twenties, early thirties maybe. I knew she had a job that required business casual dress most days but didn't really know anything else about her, other than obviously the apple fritters weren't doing her any harm; she was in great shape.

"No, I just come for the yoga class."

"I've never done yoga before," I admitted.

"You'll love it! And this instructor is great at helping beginners, so don't worry about it."

Sam and Gladys walked in, followed by an attractive woman dressed in black and lime green workout pants and a lime green tank that said "Forget diamonds, give me yoga pants" on the front. She shut the door behind her and clapped her hands.

"Okay ladies, I see some new faces today which is exciting. I'm Felicity and I'll be your instructor." She made her way to the back wall of the room, in front of the mirror.

The other women in the class took a yoga mat from the rack in the corner and begin spreading them out on the floor so we followed suit. I spread out my neon blue yoga mat between Gladys and Sam. We ended up near the front of the class, nearest to Felicity, much to my chagrin. I darted my eyes around like a cornered animal, but there were no other open spaces.

Felicity must have noticed.

"I don't think I've seen you three here before. Do you have a regular yoga practice?"

I snorted. Sam elbowed me. "We have always wanted to try it out," she told Felicity.

"Alright! You've picked a perfect day. Today our session is all about flexibility and stretching. You only take the poses as far as you are comfortable; everyone will be at different levels which is fine."

Felicity picked up her own yoga mat and rolled it out parallel to the mirror so that we could see exactly what she was doing and follow her positions.

"First, mountain pose," said Felicity, as she placed her feet together and extended her arms and fingertips down her side. "Look forward, straight in front of you; spread your toes; feel your feet grounding into the mat," she called out.

"Well, this isn't so bad," Gladys cupped her hand around her mouth and attempted to whisper. I groaned inwardly. You never, ever tell a teacher something isn't hard; it's like then it's their mission to make it hell for you. I was afraid yoga class would be no different.

"Now," Felicity continued, "elongate your arms over your head, stretch as high as you can go, and then sweep down and come into standing forward bend." I watched her move with ease and grace, coming to a stop when her forehead touched her knees and both palms were flat on the floor. And then I tried. Ha! I took comfort that I could at least see my knees when I bent forward, but my fingers barely grazed the floor and I definitely couldn't fold completely in half. A twinge in my back was already asking me if this was really necessary. From the corner of my eye, I could see that Sam wasn't much closer than I was to the goal.

"Wonderful, just perfect," chirped Felicity as she began moving around the room to check progress. She slipped a few foam blocks under my hands so that my palms rested flat on them instead of the floor. "Don't be afraid to use the yoga blocks, ladies," she told the class, passing out several more. "Back to mountain pose."

Stepping back onto her mat, Felicity joined us in mountain pose. "Watch me now. We are going to sweep down to standing forward bend, take two breaths there, and then step your feet back into a push-up position."

We all swooped and stepped after she had demonstrated. Thanks to lifting heavy bowls of batter and trays of goodies daily, my arm muscles were able to support a push-up position without much trouble. Gladys, on the other hand, was shaking like a mini-earthquake was happening under her mat.

"For those of you having trouble in this area, rest your knees on your mat as you continue to lengthen through your arms. Good. Two breaths here."

And in this way, yoga continued; we inclined to upward-facing dog, pushed ourselves in downward-facing dog, stretched into several more head-to-knee, or in many of our cases, head-to-block positions until every muscle in my body ached.

At least I wasn't the only one drenched in sweat.

"Wow, what a workout!" Sam passed me a hand-towel from a stack, using one to wipe her own forehead and neck.

"Yeah, I had no idea being flexible was such hard work."

Gladys joined us, shuffling slowly over and leaning against the wall.

"I'm worn out. I think next time, I'm leaving all this exercise stuff to you girls. I was really just hoping for one of those spicy male teachers like you see on tv, the ones with the tight pants…"

Thankfully, Felicity started speaking and we didn't get to hear the rest of Gladys's yoga fantasy.

"Remember ladies, no food or drinks other than water for thirty minutes. Your body is still in detox thanks to all the deep asanas you reached today."

I don't know what an asana is, but I was bummed about the no food part. I had just been thinking how many cookies must have been burned off during our session, and looking forward to replacing them.

Our assistants soon came to collect us. We elected to shower in our suites. I swear I've had more showers a day here than some people take in a week. As soon as I finished, I slipped into my fluffy robe and tiptoed over to Sam's room.

"We have to figure out these notes," I said, dropping to her bed with a flourish once she opened the door for me to come inside.

"Definitely," she nodded in agreement. "Here let's make a list." Sam thrust a small notebook and purple pen at me.

I was a compulsive list maker, which she knew, so I flipped to an empty page with a smile; perfect, a list would make it all clear I decided. At least I felt like I was doing something besides sitting around, waiting around for the crazy person to appear.

"The first list," I said, "places the notes have appeared." Did I mention I like lists? So, yes, there would be multiple.

"Bakery, foot massage chair, dry sauna."

"Okay," I scribbled as I talked, "second list: people who don't think I should be here. Broussard."

"Broussard's sister, my mother," Sam shrugged, "we may as well include her. You know she doesn't like anyone 'below a certain caliber' to be at the same spa she frequents."

"True," I agreed. "Oh, and Margarite – she subscribes to the same school of thought as Broussard."

"Fine. Is there a third list?"

"There is always a third list!" I beamed a wide smile at my friend as she gave me a long-suffering stare. "List number three is people with opportunity."

"Gladys."

"I don't remember Broussard, your mom, or other staff being at the bakery. Then again, we were busy and they could have sent the note to be dropped off by someone else. We were extremely busy that day."

"So, everyone goes on the list? That isn't exactly helpful, is it?"

"No," I sighed, closing my eyes in defeat.

Before we could brainstorm any further, a knock came on Sam's suite door. Gladys was standing on the other side, fully dressed and evidently ready for lunch.

"Are you two not ready yet? I thought surely I would be the old lady holding things up," she grinned.

"I guess it has been more than the required thirty minutes since we finished yoga," remarked Sam.

"Time flies," I stood up and tightened my robe. "I'll be ready in ten minutes."

"Me too."

I decided on the blue sundress to wear to lunch, tossed on a pair of flat sandals, and pulled my hair into a high ponytail on top of my head. Deodorant, a spritz of perfume, and I was ready to go. I thought to check my messages but couldn't find my phone so I decided to look at them later.

Lunch today was set up in a similar manner to yesterday. Long tables lined the garden, but today most of the foods were cold cuts and raw fruits and veggies. Obviously, they were going for lighter fare and, sadly, the decision had impacted the dessert table as well. Watermelon, berries, parfaits, and angel food cake were the healthy options today. Thank goodness there is an emergency bowl of truffles in my purse.

We passed by Belle and her mother Eloise, but their table was full today so we didn't stop. Belle smiled before continuing to move around the spinach on her plate with her fork. Note to self, maybe I should find Belle when I dip into the emergency truffle stash. The poor girl probably needed some chocolate.

Making quick work of lunch, Gladys told us she wanted to go back to the room and do her Bible study before our deep tissue massage appointment later this afternoon.

I looked wistfully at the beach which was just a short hike from the garden, down a hill and over dunes.

Jutting out my lower lip in a pout, I turned to Sam, "Want to go walk on the beach?"

"Sure, let me throw these away and I'll meet you down there."

"Okay, thanks!" I pushed in my chair as Sam cleaned up the table. It took me a moment to find the small, dirt path. I assumed jumping through the manicured hedge bordering the garden would be frowned upon, but eventually, the opening appeared and I began the climb down the gravel path, toward the rolling dunes.

It was a beautiful afternoon with temperatures in the mid-seventies, not very much of a breeze but still, it wasn't hot out. I stopped at the edge of the dunes and glanced back over my shoulder. I could see that Sam had been caught by two ladies chatting. Since it didn't look like she would be joining me anytime soon, I continued on my way to the ocean's edge. Few other people were out on this portion of the beach, though I could see small dots of people and umbrellas in the distance. I resisted the urge to wade in the gently lapping tide as it caressed the sandy shore; I wasn't aiming for another shower just yet.

I found myself lost in thought. The ocean always did that to me; its magnificence, its grandeur they both humbled and inspired me. The ocean is so much more than we can control or understand, just like life. It has dangers lurking as well, but its majestic beauty couldn't be denied.

My past held some rough patches, it would be easy to get upset about the bad in the world; there are ugly and dangerous creatures that walk on two legs as much as there are dangerous creatures that swim in the sea. Thankfully, there is also beauty in humankind – my best friend jumping in with me on a business idea, this church with members who gave up their time to serve others, all of the money raised to help and prevent future victims, the enthusiasm with which the whole community supported that cause, the beauty showed itself if you took the time to look.

I stretched my arms high above my head and closed my eyes, inhaling the salty air and the peace I found in the rhythm of the waves.

Certain that by now Jill would be looking to escort me to our massage, I began a brisk, fast walk back up the hill. Not seeing any sign of Sam in the garden, I went straight to the suites.

I wasn't prepared for the scene that greeted me when I entered the sitting room. Sam had Gladys cornered up against a wall and wouldn't let her past. Gladys was shaking her head back and forth so fast I was surprised she wasn't dizzy.

"I don't believe you. Why were you in there?" asked Sam in a raised voice, which for always calm and collected Samantha was equivalent to yelling.

"I told you, I was just looking for Piper. That's all. I was worried she might have fallen asleep and would miss the massage." Gladys responded but her eyes flitted between me, Sam, and the door to the hall.

"What in the world is going on?" I demanded.

"I saw Gladys coming out of your room when I came in here," Sam said pointing.

I raised one eyebrow and crossed my arms, waiting for Gladys to tell me what exactly she was doing in my suite.

Shuffling from one foot to the other, Gladys cast her eyes down. "I told Samantha, I was just looking in to see if you were taking a nap when you didn't answer the door."

Narrowing my eyes, I marched to my door and threw it open. At first glance, everything seemed fine, but then I remembered my missing cell phone. Suspicions whirling, I looked more closely at everything. My purse was sitting against the end of the bench instead of sitting up straight. And was that…it was. My cell phone peaked out from underneath the bed though I distinctly remember tossing it in the middle of the bed, not near an edge. Spinning to the closet, I turned the light on and gasped. My white dress had **LEAVE TOWN** smeared across it in dark, angry slashes that looked oddly like chocolate.

Wait a minute, chocolate? No! Oh, no! It couldn't be. I sprinted to my purse and dug inside, scowling when I pulled out the now empty Tupperware container. The last bits of my precious truffles, those that hadn't been sacrificed to leave nasty messages on my clothes, were smeared across the container. Now I was mad. You don't like me, fine. You want to say awful things, no problem. Threaten me and you're pushing your luck. But, take my chocolate? You have a death wish.

ELEVEN

I returned to the sitting room madder than a whole nest of hornets that had been poked with a stick, dragging the ruined dress behind me. I found Gladys and Sam sitting on opposite pieces of furniture.

"Are you knitting, right now?" I asked Gladys incredulously.

"It helps me calm down. I understand you are upset that I looked in your room for you, Piper, but I had no idea you girls would give me the third degree over it."

"I think this is more than a little upsetting, don't you?" I shoved the ruined dress in front of her. Sam inhaled sharply. Gladys dropped her knitting needles and covered her mouth with her hands, the picture of horrified, but I wasn't letting it go that easily.

"Gladys, is there something you have against me? Something you would like to say to me?"

"What do you mean Piper? Surely you don't think that I did that, do you?"

"Well, you were the only one in my room!"

"No, no I wasn't. That maid was here when I came back from lunch to have my quiet time."

"What maid?" Sam asked. "We specifically told Broussard no cleaning service while we were here and I know for a fact they haven't come to my suite because they are obligated to leave a survey card and a dark chocolate honey square in all rooms."

"None of those things were in my room either," I told them both. Though, if Sam had told me earlier about dark chocolate honey squares then I probably would have voted yes for the cleaning service.

"Well, no I don't remember having chocolate honey either when she left," Gladys said as she crinkled her eyes, looking thoughtful. "I know she said she was the maid though because I told her she nearly gave me a heart attack and she said 'Sorry ma'am, just taking out the trash' then she quickly left the room."

I looked to Sam and back at the dress. Did this mysterious person who talked to Gladys exist? Was I the "trash" she referred to?

"Come to think of it," Gladys continued as she searched the cushions for her knitting needles, "she wasn't carrying anything when she left. She did have on some of those blue plastic gloves though."

I sank down onto the couch in defeat. It sounded plausible. I didn't know what to think anymore. I genuinely liked Gladys from the moment she entered our bakery, but the timing of everything was suspicious. I was exhausted and now I had no chocolate.

"What did this lady look like, Gladys?" I asked after a moment but was robbed of a reply.

Rap, rap-tap-tap. Knocking at the door had all of us jumping. Lola opened the door this time, with Jill and Cynthia behind her. "Is everyone ready to have those sore yoga muscles worked?" she asked with a wide grin. Confusion clouded her face when her enthusiasm was met with three groans.

~

I really should have started a list, I thought to myself. A different list that is, of what was wonderful and what should never be done again at this spa. I was still on the fence about which list this deep tissue massage would make it onto. When they said deep, they meant it. There were moments I was almost asleep with the repetitive motion of the woman kneading my shoulders, and then she would nearly pull my head off with some evil neck stretching maneuver that I was fairly certain should be illegal. Maybe this was a case of pleasure outweighing the pain, but we would have to see.

On a positive note, the massage table was more like an over-fluffed, twin-size bed that was heated and felt like laying on a cloud. And they let you keep your underwear on so I was happy not being completely naked under the warm blanket.

Gladys was snoring. I kicked myself when I realized I forgot to ask again for a description of the miscreant who defiled my dress and demolished my emergency chocolate stash after we were interrupted by the knocking.

Sam was carrying on a softly spoken conversation with the woman in charge of her massage. I heard them mention "trouble spot" and "carrying extra tension" a few times and concluded this must be the person who does Sam's massage on a fairly regular basis.

My person was not a talker and that was fine with me. I had too much thinking to do to be a good conversationalist anyway.

By the time the hour session was up, massage had fully moved to my approved list. Of the many aches and pains that stretching unprepared during yoga had caused, none remained. My muscles felt like liquid, my body was so relaxed that I actually felt dizzy when I stood to step into the robe held out to me.

Sam must have seen me blinking.

She laughed, "Come on Piper, you can't have six showers and six naps a day while we're here; you're going to be worthless in the bakery next week."

I yawned widely. "I have no idea what you are even talking about," I told her.

We were escorted to the changing room where we slipped back into our regular clothes. Gladys was being very quiet; we may have hurt her feelings. I was beginning to feel bad about blaming her. The longer I thought about it during the massage, the less likely it seemed that Gladys would have any reason to hate me, much less ruin my dress and my chocolates. That seemed too immature for someone Gladys's age. Perhaps we should revisit our list soon.

The nail salon room was right next door to the changing area, so we didn't need an escort this time. We popped over and signed in at the front counter. While we waited for the girl with the goth style to set up the stations, Sam and I decided that tonight after dinner we would tell Gladys about the notes.

"We can watch her reaction," Sam said, "but I'm beginning to doubt she did it, too."

Goth girl, I should really figure out her name, walked up just then. She led us to three tables and seated us in large, plush chairs. Nail techs were seated on the other side of the small tables, in much less comfortable chairs I noticed, and an array of sparkly things were set out in front of them.

"Welcome to Bejeweled Nails!" Kim, the lady sitting at my table, spoke up. "In front of you are all of our jewels for you to choose from. You can have as many or as few as you would like."

That finally perked Gladys back up. She got so excited about the design for her nails that she either forgot about or forgave us for our accusations and interrogation of her earlier.

"Oh, look at these! Sam, you just have to get these gorgeous red gems to match your hair," she picked up a set and waved them at Sam.

Before Sam could even look at them, much less respond, Gladys's attention was captured by yet another sparkly sheet and new idea. "Piper! These are you, completely you." She pointed at a page of synthetic pearls that shimmered iridescently with hints of turquoise and light pink.

They were stunning. Okay, so maybe Gladys had a good eye. I picked up the sheet and handed it to Kim.

"These please," I told her, "in a spiral pattern on my thumbs and three in the center of my nail, vertically, for each of my other fingers."

Sam went with the red jewels suggested by Gladys.

"A heart pattern on my thumbs and one dot on each of the other fingers," she told the tech at her table.

"Well," I leaned back to ask Gladys, "what are you getting?"

"Bright pink diamonds," Gladys held up the sparkly jewels to show me.

The process took much longer than I expected, though what I based any expectation on I have no idea. We received the manicure, nail trim, and cuticle treatment before the bejeweling even began. Then it was a tedious process, as the techs had to dab a dot of clear glue onto our fingernail with a small, metal ball-tipped instrument. Next, with a tiny pair of tweezers, the jewel was peeled off the sheet and meticulously placed onto the fingernail. And then repeat the process again, one jewel at a time. I felt terrible for requesting the spiral instead of sticking to one jewel per nail, poor Kim.

It was an hour and fifteen minutes later before all of our nails were completed. I had to admit they looked pretty amazing, but bejeweling was definitely going on the "not again" list. The paint was much faster, plus I could only imagine what customers would think of finding one of these beautiful jewels in a cookie when they bite down should it fall off without me noticing. Nope, too risky for having on a regular basis.

Jill, Lola, and Cynthia were seated in the waiting area, apparently waiting on us.

"Ladies, if you don't hurry you will be late to dinner," Cynthia tut-tutted at us.

Picking up the pace, it had been a long time since lunch, after all, we returned to the suite to dress. Sam loaned me a pale pink jumpsuit. Gladys wore a frilly lace concoction that reminded me of my grandmother's Easter dress when I was a child. Sam wore a tan and blue maxi dress.

"Casual night it is?" I asked, waving my arms at our attire.

"Yes, well, it has been a long day." Gladys shrugged.

"For such a relaxing place, both of our days have been rather long so far," I couldn't help but point out.

Tap-tap, tap-tap. This time when the knock came, I was close to the door and flung it open. I don't think I will ever want an assistant for anything ever again in my life after this.

"Let me guess," I began, "you're here to collect us for dinner?"

A masculine throat cleared and I looked into the stoic face of Broussard. Instead of *look before you leap*, perhaps I should consider *look before you talk* as a new philosophy.

"Miss Lowe," he spoke around me. Literally. It was like I wasn't even standing there. I narrowed my eyes and pursed my lips but he continued without a bother. "Miss Lowe I've come to escort your party to dinner and to inform you of the good news. Margarite will return tomorrow to assist you. We hope Cynthia's service was acceptable for the interim period that was necessary."

I rolled my eyes, and even that received no notice from Broussard; maybe this guy had been part of the Queen's Guard in his past. Sam took it in stride.

"Thank you. I do believe we are ready." Then she grinned wickedly and threaded her arm through mine. "Piper, are you ready?"

I stuck my nose as far in the air as I could manage without tipping backward, "Yes, Miss Lowe, I am quite famished. Let us proceed." She bit her lip to contain the laughter bubbling to the surface.

Not to be outdone, Gladys strolled past us and grabbed hold of Broussard's starched elbow. "Well, don't just stand there," she said cheekily, "escort me to dinner, sir."

Broussard turned the color of a ripe tomato, but he did not remove Gladys and indeed escorted her all the way to the dining hall. Unable to bite back the laughter any longer, Sam tried to mask it with a long, fake coughing spell.

If nothing else, I thought as we walked, this spa trip was much less boring than I imagined it would be.

Much to our surprise, Belle joined us at dinner that evening.

"Mother has a headache," she explained. "Her friend Winnie was kind enough to sit with her and they bid me go to dinner and not worry about Mother. Really, I think they had gossip they decided was too juicy for me to hear."

"Well we are glad you joined us, dear," Gladys patted her hand.

"Do you live near here?" I asked Belle.

She shook her head, swallowing the bite of salmon she had just put in her mouth.

"No. We come for a long weekend two or three times a year. We live in Rock Pointe, a few hours north of here."

We chatted about her home, the town, and the church for a short time. It was a pleasant enough conversation, but I was struggling to pay attention. With the prospect of dessert looming, my thoughts skipped back to the ruined dress and ruined chocolates. Now that the initial shock and fury had passed, I also had to admit to myself that the thought of someone in my suite and going through my things gave me chills.

Sam and Belle decided to split the strawberry cheesecake so I asked Gladys to share the molten lava cake and ice cream. The liquid chocolate assuaged some of my fear, but I was still antsy. Sam noticed and called an end to our evening.

"Belle, I think we are going to turn in for the night but please, do find us sometime tomorrow. It was a pleasure chatting with you tonight."

"Thank you," Belle smiled, scooting her chair back to stand up. "I'm sure I should be checking on Mother now anyway. Who knows, maybe I'll be in time to catch some tidbits of news to share with you tomorrow."

After we had arrived back at the suite, Sam lay down on the floor staring at the ceiling. Gladys took up a seat in a wingback chair. I stretched my legs out in front of me on the divan.

"Gladys, you never got to tell us what the woman coming from my room, claiming to be the maid, looked like."

"That's right. Let me think."

"Anything you remember would help. We are trying to find out who is doing all of this."

"She was a bit shorter. Blonde hair. Wait, what do you mean all of this? I thought we were trying to figure out who ruined your beautiful dress?"

Sam rolled to a sitting position and looked at me.

Sighing, I started at the beginning.

"And so, you see why we were suspicious when Sam found you coming out of my room," I shrugged after I explained about the location and nature of the notes that had been left so far.

"I promise you," Gladys leaned forward in her chair, looking me straight in the eyes, "I didn't do any of those things, Piper."

"Who else was on our list?" Sam asked.

I closed my eyes, trying to recall the names we had written down. "Broussard. Broussard's sister whose name I can't remember. Your mother, who I doubt would ever willingly smear her hands in chocolate. Margarite."

"It was definitely not Margarite I saw leaving your room today," Gladys said, adding thoughtfully, "though whoever it was looked vaguely familiar."

"So that is two we can take off the list," Sam tapped her chin thoughtfully. "We have to add one other though."

"Who?"

"The unknown suspect for the unknown reason. What? Don't look at me like I'm kooky. I saw it on a detective show once."

"Fine. And if it were Broussard, he had to have an accomplice because Gladys clearly saw a blonde woman."

Gladys yawned.

"Me too," Sam said. "Let's call it a night."

"Agreed. We can plan our appointments for tomorrow when we get up in the morning," I said as I stood and stretched.

We each departed to our own suites, I turned off the sitting room light as I went. Changing into my pajamas, I crawled underneath the covers and slipped my kindle out of the nightstand drawer. At this point in my book, the maiden had agreed for the knight to journey with her to the other side of the haunted forest. This was not for her protection, she told him, but he was handy at setting up camp and she could spend more time hunting for supper while it was still daylight that way.

I was considering putting the story down for the night. My drooping eyelids were becoming rather persistent when my text message beep sounded from my purse where I had dropped my phone earlier.

I powered down the kindle before crawling to the foot of the bed and digging out my phone. Plopping back onto my pillows, I got comfortable again before swiping through the lock screen to see who was texting me.

Griff: Hey
Me: What?
Griff: Were you sleeping?
Me: Not yet.

Griff: How's the spa?

Me: Exhausting.

Griff: You sure you are at the spa???

Me: :-/

Griff: Did you figure out the clothes?

Me: Why?

Griff: Curious, you seemed stressed about it.

Me: Got worse.

Honestly, I don't even know why I am telling Griff. Heck, I don't even know why he is texting me, but I'm tired and exhausted and don't have the energy to question it.

Griff: What did?

Me: The clothes.

Griff: How?

Me: Someone ruined my last dress.

Me, after several moments of silence: It doesn't matter, it's fine.

Me: I think I'm going to go to bed.

Griff: Okay. Tomorrow will be better Piper.

Me: Whatever you say.

I turned my phone on silent and plugged it into the charger. Sleep came much easier than I expected. Staying asleep was harder. I tossed and turned trying to escape the flapping notes chasing me in my dreams.

TWELVE

I awoke slowly the next morning. I vaguely recalled strange dreams, but not the details of any of them. I looked at the clock on my phone. 7 AM. Wow, I was really getting the hang of this sleeping in thing! In fact, I might need to worry about how hard getting back into my early-morning schedule at the bakery might be when this trip is over.

Knowing by now that most of the appointments at the spa didn't begin until nine in the morning, I decided to take my time getting ready. I ran hot water in the large garden tub and added some bubble bath. Grabbing my Kindle, and a towel, I eased into the warm water and continued reading where I left off last night.

When the water began to cool and my skin was getting wrinkly, I shut down the Kindle and climbed out. A few quick braids to my hair would have to do today because I had run out of time to blow dry it. I shrugged into my robe and tightened the belt around my middle before going to check on my suitemates. Sure enough, I found them in the sitting room.

"Piper," Gladys greeted me, raising a mug in my direction.

"What's this?" I asked sinking into a plush, purple chair and accepting the drink.

"Hot chocolate, extra creamy."

I inhaled the rich scent.

"Yum!"

It was divine; never had I drank such a luscious hot chocolate.

"Wow! This is wonderful," I wiped a chocolate mustache on my arm, not at all self-conscious. I would wear the mustache all day if it meant I got to keep drinking this.

Sam nodded in agreement, up to her nose in her own mug, whether it was of chocolate or coffee I wasn't certain until she came up for air sporting a matching chocolate line along her upper lip.

"Can I please send a picture to your mother?" I asked laughing. "Wait, it could be your Christmas card!"

"Brilliant though that might be," Sam shook her head, "no, you may not send anyone my picture like this. I haven't even brushed my hair yet."

"Fine," I pouted. "So, what are we doing today?"

"Well, our nails and toes are done for the week," Gladys pointed out, wiggling her Lucifer tipped toes at us.

"I have some thoughts," Sam said. "Since Piper never got to fully experience the chocolate face mask, we should give a facial another try. I saw a few on here that sounded good."

"I can live with that," I told her, nodding that she should continue.

"The first is a cleansing, steam and conch-shell scrub. They take a combination of small, crushed-up pieces of conch shells and an oil of your choice mixed together. It is said to be an amazing exfoliant, without scratching or damaging your skin because of the soft, powder-like substance of the crushed shell."

"What is the other?" I asked. That sounded like a fairly extensive process to me.

"The other is a gold facial."

"A what?"

"A gold facial. Cream that contains gold is applied to our face for a certain amount of time before removal and is supposed to improve radiance, elasticity, and complexion. Plus, they put gold on your face, how much more pampered can you get?"

Gladys and I agreed that those both sounded excellent.

"Anything else?" Gladys asked her.

"I assumed nobody was ready to go back to yoga class," Sam waited for our nods of confirmation. "There is still another class offered here. It involves food."

"Yes."

"You don't' even know what it is yet, Piper."

"Food. Yes."

Gladys shrugged, "Whatever you think, Sam."

Sam pushed the intercom button and Margarite appeared. Sam relayed our choices for the day and Margarite disappeared down the hallway.

Sam brought me a short jumpsuit of hers to wear; she dressed in a smart skirt and blouse. Gladys was a little miffed that we decided robes weren't appropriate today since we wouldn't need to undress for anything. She opted for black, velour lounge pants and a pink top.

Margarite, Lola, and Jill arrived promptly at five 'til nine to escort us to the facial appointments.

As we were walking, I thought I saw a blonde head peer around a corner and disappear back out of sight, but when we got to that spot, not a soul was in the hallway or the attaching corridor. Maybe my nerves were a bit frayed.

"Oh!" Gladys exclaimed, "I forgot something in the room. I'll catch right back up, go on."

I paused, watching her retreating figure.

"I think I'll go make sure I unplugged my curling iron," Sam gave as an excuse to follow her. I knew my friend must have sensed my lingering unease with Gladys's continued trips alone to our rooms and I was grateful.

Margarite scowled. I got the impression that she was easily upset with anything that interfered with her schedule.

Jill led me the rest of the way to get ready for our facials. Jan was noticeably absent; I briefly wondered if she were avoiding my session because of her nose.

"Not at all," Jill assured me when I voiced the concern. "Because so many of the staff here volunteer their services, we rotate out frequently. Jan had work to do at her actual office today, paying clients she was scheduled to see there."

That made sense. I settled into my chair to wait. Much to my surprise, I was joined by Belle.

"Hi, Piper."

"Good morning Belle. Are you here for a facial too?"

"Yes. Samantha sent a note through her assistant this morning asking me to join your group. Mother agreed when she learned how important Sam's parents are."

"Well, at least they are good for something," I joked.

The estheticians, or facial experts of the day whatever their job title, were busy setting up their stations. Gladys and Sam made their way in a few minutes later and one of the ladies approached us.

"Hello! What kind of oils would you ladies like mixed into your exfoliating conch-shell scrub? We have lavender, hemp, rose, eucalyptus, and tea tree oils. You are welcome to smell of any that you would like."

"Lavender would be lovely," Sam smiled.

"May I smell the lavender and the rose please ma'am," Belle, soft and shy, responded when the lady looked to her.

"Of course!" Two small, dark-colored vials were brought over for Belle to smell.

After giving it considerable thought, Belle decided on the rose scent.

Now it was my turn.

"Tea tree oil will be fine," I remembered hearing good things about it several years ago but couldn't remember the specific details.

"Yes, Miss Rivers," the woman said as she returned the other vials to the counter. "Tea Tree oil is very popular right now. And now Mrs. Hill, what oil would you like to use today?"

"Hemp," Gladys clapped her hands. I suppressed an eye roll thinking yet again that she must have been a real handful in her younger days.

With oils chosen and exfoliants mixed, the four women got started cleaning our faces. Working up a nice lather, they washed and rinsed us. Next came a hot, steamy towel wrapped around our face. It felt rather nice. Finally, the bowls of prepared crushed shell were brought over. Wearing gloves, the woman with my scrub smeared it in small circles all over my face until it was a thick-layer of the seashell mask. I was afraid to open my eyes or mouth even a little in case some were to get in there.

"Now, we leave the masks on for one minute and then we will come back and rinse everything off," one of the women said.

"It kind of itches," Gladys mumbled.

"Don't touch it," someone told her.

One minute, I learned, seemed to take quite a long time. When at last our faces were devoid of powdery seashell bits, we were given bottles of water to drink and asked to wait a few more moments while the second portion of today's facials, the gold masks, were made ready.

Peeking in the bowl as it was brought over to my chair, I had to admit it was a gorgeous shade of gold; bright and shiny.

"Would you take our photo after?" I asked.

"Yes, I can do that." I handed my phone to the lady to use after she was finished with my face. The paste had been warmed up, thank goodness because the crushed shell powder had been so cold, and it felt wonderful as she painted it over my face with a large brush.

"Okay, smile for the camera!"

The four of us posed, smiled, and laughed.

"Now, this mask must sit for twelve minutes. We will return to peel it off for you at that time." With that, the four women left the room, leaving us sitting in our chairs with nothing to do.

"Belle," Samantha began, "did you interrupt any good gossip when you went back to your mother's suite last night?"

"Just a little," the girl responded with a shrug, "a celebrity is staying here all of next week but I don't know who it is. And then they were discussing your brother getting married but you wouldn't want to hear all of that."

"I'm sorry," Sam said, "whose brother is getting married?"

"Yours. Griffith, Griff something."

"Um no. Griffin isn't even dating anyone right now. That can't be right."

"I'm positive that's what Mother and Winnie were saying. Some girl with political ambitions that Deidra believes can bring her son back from the dark side and into his role for Mayor after your father steps down several years from now."

"That doesn't even make sense. Mayors are elected, first of all. You can't just decide who is going to get the job."

"Well, actually," I told Sam, "the rumor would make complete sense if it were coming from your mom. She thinks she can get her way about everything; one little election wouldn't stand in her way. Still, I agree with you that surely Griff would have at least told you if he were seeing someone."

Our conversation halted as the women came back in to remove our gold masks. Working slowly, they peeled the mask a little at a time so it came off in the shape of our faces. The sensation it created along my skin was tingly, and stretched it, but felt good; almost like I could feel it pulling dirt from each pore as it left. Disgusting and fascinating at the same time.

Our gold skins were thrown away and we were handed sample-sized moisturizers.

"Oh look, tea tree oil," I said.

"Mine is rose," Belle held up her bottle for me to see.

"You have each been given moisturizers made with the same oil you chose for your scrub. If you would like something different you may let me know," said the lady who seemed to be the authority of the group and did all of the talking.

"Nope, this will be just fine," Gladys held the bottle to her nose and inhaled. Oh boy.

They showed us how to apply the moisturizer to our faces in small, gentle circles before declaring our facial session complete.

"Thank you," I called over my shoulder as we exited the room and followed our gang of personal assistants back to our suite.

"Belle, we would love for you to join us. Margarite, please order tea be brought to our sitting room," Sam said in one fluid breath; there was no time for anyone to object.

~

Settled into various cushions, chairs, and divans, Gladys offered to pour tea for everyone We had dismissed Jill and Lola, who had delivered the tea on a quaint little cart with a full tea service including sugar, cream, and shortbread cookies with cups and saucers for everyone. Linen napkins were folded in the shapes of seashells.

"Thumbprint cookies! It has been so long since I've had these," I reached for one of the round cookies that had a dollop of the red jam in the indentation in the center. "Yum, raspberry," I said while licking my lips.

"I got blackberry-flavored," Belle smiled.

Sam munched on a regular shortbread with no jam.

"Sam!" I startled her with my sudden light-bulb moment, "We can make peanut butter and jelly cookies at the bakery with peanut butter soft cookies, thumb-printed to hold grape jelly."

"Thumb-printed?" she arched one eyebrow high above the other.

"You're welcome, it is a new word, so use it."

"Fine, we can make peanut butter and jelly thumbprints. Now, back to the reason we are here…Belle, I'm having trouble wrapping my mind around this rumor that my brother is getting married. Start over, if you don't mind."

"Okay," Belle agreed, sipping from her teacup before she began. "I let myself into the suite with as little noise as possible, taking time to close the door gently. My slippers were inside the entrance, so I traded out my heels for the soft, silent slippers right away. I didn't exactly sneak up on Mother and Winnie. That would be rude, but I didn't call out or announce myself either. You never learn the good stuff that way, and my mother treats me as if I'm still twelve and not ready for the adult world."

Sam nodded sympathetically as I rolled my eyes at parents in general, thinking of how Sam's mother still tried to plan her entire life rather than trusting the choices Sam made for herself. Encouraged by our reactions, Belle continued.

"Winnie was speaking and as she has a rather loud, whiny voice. She was easy to hear from the entry while I hung up my shawl. 'It's too bad about that Griffin Lowe boy,' she was telling Mother. 'He would have been a fine catch for your Belle, political connections and all.'"

I burst out laughing, "A fine catch? Poor Belle, do they think dating is a simple sport of fishing for the big one? What about friendship, love, respect, or maybe actually knowing the person first?"

"I know, I swear my mother is Elizabeth Bennett's mother reincarnated."

"'Daughters, married'," Sam quoted in a fit of silent laughter, wiping tears from her eyes.

"Don't mind these two," Gladys flapped her hands at us impatiently, "keep going with your story."

"Mother asked questions about the Lowe family and finally got around to asking who Griffin was planning to marry and if Winnie was certain it was serious. I think she was developing the idea of arranging a meeting between us!" Belle's cheeks burned scarlet but whether from embarrassment or anger it was difficult to tell. "Thankfully, that idea was nipped early on because Winnie said that it was as good as certain, that she heard it from the bride-to-be herself who was here yesterday ordering sample desserts. That is when she said that the girl was thrilled to have gained Deidra's trust in several political matters and was sure she would be grateful to have a daughter-in-law who wasn't going to let Griffin throw his life away on some common girl and common life."

"That doesn't sound like someone Griff would be into at all," Sam tapped her finger on her chin. "It's too bad that Piper and I agreed we are having an electronic free weekend or I would be tempted to call him right now."

"Yeah, that is umm," I swallowed and hoped my face wasn't heating up as quickly as Belle's had, "yes, definitely too bad you can't talk to Griff. No phones and all."

"Well I didn't agree to any no phone rule," Gladys disappeared into her suite too fast for me to puzzle out her words. When she returned to the sitting room, a glittery purple cell phone was pressed to her ear. "Yep, yep, that is what I thought. Okay, thanks, you have a nice day, dear."

THIRTEEN

Placing the phone on the table, Gladys raised her teacup to her lips and drank. Then, sitting it back down and folding her hands in her lap, she said, "Griff isn't engaged to anyone. Says somebody has lost their mind."

Sam and I gaped at Gladys.

"Oh okay," Belle said, reaching for another cookie and unaware of the confusion muddling mine and Sam's brains.

"You called Griff?" I asked as I regained control of my faculties.

"When did you get his number?" Sam cocked her head sideways in a puzzled fashion.

Gladys shrugged as she reached for a shortbread.

"Oh, just the other day at the bakery. He seemed like such a nice young man."

A knock came at the door. I shuffled over to answer it since my chair was closest.

"Hi Piper," Jill handed me a folded piece of paper and I inhaled sharply, "Belle's mother asked this be delivered to her," she finished and I felt foolish. Was I going to jump at the sight of all paper now? We really had to get to the bottom of my not-so-biggest fan. I handed the note to Belle.

Her smile fell, "I have to get back to Mother. She needs me to help her choose outfits for lunch."

"Don't worry," I patted her on the shoulder, "we'll break you out again soon."

Gladys clapped, "Oh! A jailbreak, how exciting."

"That isn't exactly what I meant," I tried to say but Belle simply snickered and turned from the room.

"Come on you two nuts, we may as well get going to lunch, too," Sam admonished us as she got up and headed to her suite to freshen up.

Gladys rang for Lola on the intercom and let her know the tea things could be collected. I was relieved that Lola came herself while we were still in the room; I had been worrying over another unknown maid perhaps coming in after we left for lunch in the garden and ruining something else of mine. With that thought on my mind, I got up and excused myself to my suite. Locking up my purse in the safe made me feel better. I returned to the sitting room just as Sam exited her suite as well.

"Ready?" Gladys asked us.

"Ready," Sam agreed. "Though I probably ate enough cookies to count for lunch just now."

I shook my head, "Negative. Those were appetizers."

~

I wiped my mouth, folded my napkin onto the table and slumped back in my chair. Not exactly fancy spa garden lunch posture but boy was I full.

"I'm stuffed bigger than a Thanksgiving turkey," Gladys echoed my thoughts with her own unique turn of phrase.

"I told you I ate too many cookies," Sam groaned.

"Watch your mouth, there is no such thing!" I reprimanded her with mock horror.

"What did we schedule for this afternoon? Please tell me it was a nap?" Gladys asked.

Sam pursed her lips in thought, "No, but I can't seem to remember either thanks to this food coma. You know what, I see Margarite hovering nearby so I will just go ask her our schedule."

Gladys stood after Sam, saying she was going to use the restroom off of the foyer. I was left sitting alone. My eyes drifted closed.

A throat cleared next to me.

"Sorry," Jill apologized as my eyes popped open in surprise. "I guess they should change my job title to mail carrier," she said with an eye-roll as she handed me an elegant looking card. "This is for you."

"Thanks," I said as I accepted the card. There was no envelope, no to or from address on the outside. I opened it not having any idea what to expect and was caught off guard by the block print newspaper letters pasted inside. **TIME IS ALMOST UP** it said.

"Jill, Jill!" I dashed after her but she was already out of my sight. I spun in circles, eyeing everyone in the crowded garden, noting all of the blonde women. Blonde heads to the right and left. I spun, blondes behind and in front of me. Was my stalker so near? Had I seen the blue-eyed woman in yoga gear in the bakery before? The older grandmother with the dye job trying to pass as two generations younger? Maybe it was the blonde in the buffet line? Or did Gladys make up the story about the blonde to throw me off track? She was noticeably absent again, but I couldn't imagine anything she would have against me. Then again, she was an odd duck and we hadn't known her long. I thought back to her conversation with the palm trees in her backyard.

Someone grabbed my arm and I clenched my fist, jerking away. "Piper?" Sam's eyes were huge. "What is wrong, didn't you hear me calling your name?"

"Sorry. Here. Read this." I watched as Sam's frown deepened as she read the note and took in the ransom-like presentation of cut and pasted letters. She stuffed it in her pocket. "Whoever is doing this is obviously a coward and possibly delusional."

"That isn't comforting. Is that supposed to be comforting?"

"No, I'm just saying don't let it get to you, Piper. We will keep our eyes open and stick together from now on. Whoever it is hasn't approached you and hopefully, they won't. Maybe they just get a kick out of messing with people."

Gladys materialized at our side. "Samantha, was Margarite able to refresh your memory on our next appointment?"

"About that…" Sam trailed off and rolled her eyes up to the sky, throwing in duck lips for good measure.

"Spill it," I told her, recognizing the bad news face.

"Yes, Margarite has our appointment set up already. We chose the food class this morning, remember."

My stomach rumbled in protest.

"I can't eat another bite!" Gladys yelped.

"Me neither," Sam said, "but I don't think we have to eat. From what I gathered out of Margarite's broken description, this is a class teaching you beauty tips and tricks as related to foods."

"Fine," I said. "But I may skip supper and just have dessert tonight."

"Don't you mean skip dessert?" Gladys asked.

"Of course not, I mean skip supper. I don't have room for any more food but the dessert in the dining hall has been decadent. I refuse to miss out on any tonight."

"Come on," Sam grabbed my hand. "Margarite and the merry assistants are waiting to escort us to the kitchen for our class."

"Piper, there you are," Jill held out a white, square box that was tied with a silver, velvety cord. "This package was delivered for you today."

"Really?" I asked accepting the package. "Who is it from?"

Jill looked down and wrung her hands together. "There was a card…I'm sorry. I bumped into some blonde woman in the hall and dropped the box. She handed it back but I was halfway down the hall before realizing the card was no longer attached. I went back to look for it; the card was nowhere to be found. I was hoping you were expecting it and wouldn't need the card."

"No, I have no idea what it could be."

"Should I take it to your suite instead?"

"I'll take it. Thank you anyway but now I'm curious to open this mysterious box."

Sam piped in, "Piper, I'm going to come with you. Just in case…"

I nodded. Sam was obviously worried that my stalker had a more sinister game in mind, escalating from notes to gifts. All the more reason to open this in private and not in an exposed place; there was no telling what might be inside.

"What's going on?" Gladys asked as she shuffled closer.

"Piper received an unexpected gift," Sam pointed at the box.

"And there was a blonde woman in the hall." Okay, that sounded lame even as I said it. Still, I found it bizarre that a blonde had a run-in with my package and now the card was missing.

"We're going to open it in the suite really quickly before we head to the food class in the kitchen."

"Okay, let's go." Gladys looked at us both, "I'm going with you…I did not send this box or any notes and I want to see what is inside, now scoot."

After assuring Jill, Margarite, and Lola that we did not need an escort to our rooms, we agreed to let them come get us in ten minutes to walk us to the kitchen since we hadn't been to that part of the spa yet. It was somewhere near the dining hall but we knew it wasn't worth the time to argue with Margarite.

I placed the box on the coffee table in the sitting room. Sam took off one of her heels and held it up.

"What are you doing?" I asked.

"Getting ready for whatever is in that box," she replied matter-of-factly. It was a good feeling to know your friend was willing to save you from any kind of attack, even if her only weapon was a shoe.

Gladys shook her head, "I doubt it can be that bad. Just open it."

So, I did. With deliberate movements I pulled the silver cord loose from the beautiful bow it was tied in, letting it fall to the table. Placing one hand on each side of the box, I braced myself and took a step back as I yanked off the lid. Nothing jumped out, fell out, or moved so I stepped back to the table and peered in the box. And gasped.

Sam raised her heel higher.

"What? What?" She and Gladys approached as I reached into the box.

With extreme care, I lifted out the most beautiful dress I had ever seen. It was simply stunning as I held it up and the whole garment was revealed. Silver, the same color as the cord, a floor length, halter-top, fitted gown. The plunging neckline glittered with Swarovski crystals that tapered off and ran down one side to the hip. The three of us simply gawked at it.

"Sam, did you buy me this?" I asked when I found my power of speech again. I was pretty sure I knew the answer since Sam was standing beside me staring, having dropped her shoe in surprise moments ago.

"No way. You would kill me if I bought you something that fancy. I'd certainly like to send a thank you note to whoever did though. Piper, this dress is going to be magnificent on you."

"Is it even my size?" I pulled the beautiful dress close and searched for the tag. Yep, my size.

"What are you standing here for?" Gladys asked. "We have about two minutes until that Margarite woman shows up at the door demanding we stop dilly-dallying around. Go try it on for goodness sake."

"Gladys is right, hurry up." Sam slipped her shoe back on her foot. "I'll search the tissue paper for any card, note, or store name."

I went to my suite and laid the silver dress across the bed. Wow. It was gorgeous but also driving me crazy that I had no idea who or where it came from. Tossing my clothes to the side, I stepped into the dress and tied the straps in a bow at the base of my neck. I had to see it before I could go show Sam or Gladys. It probably looked ridiculous. I stepped in front of the mirror in the bathroom. The dress was perfect. It fit like a glove.

"Come on, I want to see it!" Samantha's shout from the sitting room drug me from the mirror. She and Gladys were both standing at my door when I opened it.

"Piper, it's magnificent!" Sam grabbed my shoulders and spun me so she could see the whole thing.

"I knew it," Gladys said.

"What?" I asked.

"Oh, I just mean I knew it would be beautiful when you pulled it out of that box. And it is. Okay, let's get moving." Gladys clapped her hands at me. I wonder if she were ever a teacher or something. She sure did like to give orders.

After changing back, I brought the dress out on a hanger and handed it to Sam.

"Please keep this in your closet for me. I would hate for anything to happen to it."

An all too familiar knock tapped on the door. Sam rushed to get the dress put away. Margarite set a fast pace as she led us to the kitchen, all the while frowning and muttering in Spanish.

We made it on time…but just barely.

~

"Bonsoir mesdames. Je m'appelle Chef Fabio et c'est un plaisir de vous apprendre dans ma cuisine."

"Je suis Samantha," Sam responded. "English please?"

"Oui. Of course. Good evening beautiful ladies. My name is Chef Fabio and it is a pleasure to teach you in my kitchen."

Gladys fanned herself, staring at the rugged Frenchman like a hunk of beef. *Just how long had her husband Harold been deceased now*, I tried to remember but failed.

FOURTEEN

I will give Chef Fabio credit. He continued on in a very professional manner and ignored the looks of lust that several others in the class were giving him. Personally, I didn't see what all the fuss was about. Fabio was in admittedly good shape, probably in his late thirties, he appeared bald even beneath the tall chef hat he wore. Perhaps it was the accent that had everyone flustered. I guess he just wasn't my type. A pair of dark eyes flashed through my mind, but I pushed those aside and focused on the introduction.

"Today we will be learning about the beauty benefits of several foods. Who is ready to begin?" Hands shot into the air. Besides the three of us, there were six other women in the room. I was sad not to see Belle anywhere. She must still be with her mother. I recognized a couple of faces as infrequent customers but didn't know much about them since they weren't regulars. The other four I didn't know at all.

"Bien. Good. First, we have the healthy fat: avocados. Does anyone like avocados?"

I nudged Sam when she didn't raise her hand, knowing full well she loved avocados and guacamole. Personally, I didn't even want to touch the disgusting things.

"I told you," she said, "I can't eat another bite right now."

Chef Fabio continued talking as he expertly pitted and sliced one avocado into six pieces and handed them out to anyone wishing to partake on small plates with appetizer forks.

"Not only is avocado a source of healthy fat, but it also contains biotin. What does biotin do ladies?"

"It is great for hair and nail growth," Sam answered when Chef Fabio nodded in her direction.

"Bien, Samantha. Biotin prevents brittle nails and hair. A less discussed benefit of biotin is the hydration it can provide for dry skin." There were murmurs of interest from a few ladies.

"Next on the list, we have the beautiful pomegranate." With an added flourish that I feared would cause a few swoons, Chef Fabio reached beneath the counter where he stood and tossed two pomegranates in the air before catching them. A smattering of claps sounded, most of them coming from Gladys. I gave Sam the eye and she shrugged, mouthing a silent "sorry" my direction.

As Chef Fabio proceeded to cut each pomegranate in half he asked, "Who has never tried this excellent and exotic fruit?"

My hand decided to betray me, raising halfway in the air even as my brain tried to tell it that I was much too full to consider taste-testing right now. Too late. Chef Fabio pointed my direction and then to a woman to my right.

"Come on over here ladies and enjoy a sample." Chef Fabio handed us each a small bowl, smaller than a souffle dish, that he had scooped a spoonful of the little red seeds into. "These jewels of the pomegranate are magnificent, here tell me what you think."

I tipped a spoon of five or six seeds into my mouth. Bad idea. I shuddered a little and was relieved to see Chef Fabio placing several bottles of water on the counter. Trading my bowl of seeds for one of those bottles, I twisted off the lid and gulped. Sam was shaking with silent mirth.

"It tastes almost like cranberries but a little different," I told Chef Fabio before drinking more water.

"Odd," the other woman said, "I was thinking they tasted kind of like a cherry."

"You are both correct," Chef Fabio looked pleased as punch, and no I've never understood that phrase but my mom used it all the time and I think it is now in my DNA. "Depending on the ripeness and the variety of pomegranate, they can taste similar to both of those things. To tell the fruit is ripe, it should feel very heavy when you hold it and the skin should be taught."

"And what good is pomegranate for beauty, Chef?" Gladys asked.

"Pomegranate provides a plethora of benefits due to its richness in anti-oxidants. Collagen production is promoted, immunity is improved, it can even enhance the circulation of your blood."

Gladys fanned herself faster with the napkin.

"Next on our list are walnuts."

Now walnuts I knew about; I love walnuts. Bonus for me was the omega-3 fatty acids they contained but I didn't actually remember why omega-3 was good for beauty.

"Those have omega-3s, right?" One of the ladies who I'd seen at Ooey-Gooey-Goodness once or twice spoke up from the back.

"Oui, bien. Yes, good. The omega-3 fatty acids in walnuts contribute to a glowing and youthful appearance for the skin. Walnuts are wonderful to snack on alone but they are also quite versatile. Walnuts can be added to anything from a simple salad to a crusted-chicken entrée, or even a magnificent dessert." Chef Fabio and I seemed to share a love of walnuts I gathered based on this glowing delivery of their uses. Maybe the man knows his stuff after all.

"I would now like to talk to you about another extra special ingredient. Emphasis on the extra. Do we have any guesses?" Chef Fabio straightened his collar as he waited.

Unfortunately for him, there didn't seem to be any prodigies in the class today. Giving up, Chef Fabio reached beneath the counter again and pulled out a large glass bottle.

"Extra Virgin Olive Oil!"

A collection of "ohhhs" and "ahhhs" filled the room and Chef Fabio took a small bow. "Yes, this magic bottle is the healthiest of cooking oils. It also contains good fatty acids and a large quantity of anti-oxidant polyphenols. Both go a long way in providing a youthful glow and protection for the skin from some harmful molecules called free radicals."

I leaned around Gladys to whisper to Sam, "So are we supposed to eat it or rub it on our face?"

"Be sure to check out the salad on tonight's dinner menu; you will see a lot of things you recognize," Chef Fabio was telling us when suddenly a blaring alarm sounded and the sprinkler system activated.

The ladies around us started shrieking, whether from fear of a fire or despair of a ruined outfit I couldn't be certain. I didn't see any smoke yet, but we all began filing towards the emergency exit as fast as we could maneuver around the counter and each other. Chef Fabio I noticed had dashed out without a backward glance at the class full of women.

As we tripped and stumbled outside, I could see that the smoke was coming out of the yoga studio window. Firetrucks came careening into the parking lot, men in thick suits filing out. Several entered the building while others began unrolling the hose. They were just hooking it up to the fire hydrant when two of the firefighters exited the building.

"False alarm," one shouted, holding up a round object above his head. The other few firemen also came out of the building, also holding small objects. Smoke continued to pour from the building.

They huddled together with Pastor Dan. The men on the truck began rolling the hose back up.

"What's going on?" I asked nobody in particular.

"I'm not sure," Sam answered, "but I'm definitely going to find out." She began making her way through the crowd toward the group of firefighters. "Excuse me, pardon me," she inched her way forward but it was slow going.

I turned, then realized we had lost Gladys somewhere in the scuffle to get out of the building. I scanned the crowd, looking for her familiar face when another person flashed into my view.

The same person I thought I saw at lunch in the garden the first day. A nagging feeling started up inside me. What in the world was she doing at the spa instead of at work multiple days this week?

I decided to go ask.

Pushing past several groups of people clustered together and talking animatedly, I caught up with her.

FIFTEEN

"Samantha!" Gladys panted. "Sam!" she yelled again.

"Gladys?" Sam turned away from Pastor Dan and the fireman she was speaking with at the sound of her name. "Oh! My goodness, Gladys! Are you okay?"

Panting Gladys nodded but didn't speak.

Sam reached out to the firefighter and jerked a water bottle from his hand as he turned to answer a yell from his buddy. The look of startled surprise on his face would have been amusing if Sam hadn't been concerned that Gladys was about to be seriously ill.

"Are you okay?" Sam asked again. "Here drink this."

Gladys chugged half the bottle, coughing and sputtering afterward.

"Did you inhale smoke Gladys?" Pastor Dan asked in a voice laced with concern as he patting her on the back.

"I'm fine. It's Piper," she pointed. "Something happened to Piper."

Pastor Dan and Sam shared a look of alarm.

"What happened to Piper?" Sam asked.

"The fire was a false alarm," Pastor Dan said. "Was she hurt in the rush from the building?"

"Oh! Was she trampled like you see at all of those horrible holiday sales where people pay no attention to others around them?" Sam scanned the crowd as she turned her head left and right, desperate for a view of her friend.

"No. Piper was taken. In a van," Gladys finally regained her breath enough to talk in full sentences. She took another swallow of water and screwed the cap on tight.

"I was trying to get out of the crowd of panicking people. I saw a nice bench beneath a beautiful palm tree. I was almost to it when I heard this loud bang. I looked over and saw Piper being dragged into the back of a van by some blonde woman. She looked so familiar that I knew she must have been the one in our suite but for the life of me I still have no idea who she is," Gladys sighed with frustration.

"Sam, what's going on?" Griff joined the three of them. "I saw all the firetrucks. Is everyone okay? Where's Piper? I really need to talk to her. Is she mad at me for buying the dress? I bet she is. I really need to see her."

"Griff!" Sam nearly sobbed as she latched onto her big brother. "Griff, thank God you're here. Piper's gone."

"Gone?" Griff stiffened.

"Not gone," Pastor Dan clarified. "But she is missing, son. Call 911. Gladys, please, finish telling us everything you can."

"I couldn't see what was on the white van that the woman pulled Piper into. Then I remembered my phone could take pictures so I pulled it out of my pocket. Here look, I got the license plate!" Gladys dropped the phone in her haste.

Picking it up, she wiped the dirt off and clicked her Gallery icon.

"Nope. Thumb. Grass. Nope. Wait! Here it is," Gladys held the phone out.

Griff grabbed the phone and gave the license plate number to dispatch.

"Units are on route here and they put out a news bulletin on the license number," Griff told them as he hung up the phone.

Sam grabbed Gladys's phone, did something quickly, and gave it back. Then she typed like a madwoman on the keypad of her own phone.

"What are you doing?" Gladys asked trying to peer over Sam's shoulder.

"I just posted that van license photo on Facebook. Forget waiting for the police! I'm going to find Piper. We have to," she clenched her fists as tears rolled down her cheeks.

"Sam," Gladys reached out and took the younger girl's hands in her own. "Sam, I'm so worried. Piper wasn't moving when she was being loaded into that van."

Wringing his hands through his hair, Griff let out a deep growl. Gladys and Sam looked at him in surprise.

"No. It can't be. Not Piper. Not Abigail. Why?" Griff began pacing and mumbling barely coherent sentences to himself. "Who even thinks up arranged marriages anyway. She isn't so cruel. She couldn't be. She just had a crush, nothing big really. Abigail is not going to hurt Piper. This is all my fault! How could I be so stupid?"

Sam was about to ask what he was talking about when the police showed up.

One of them had two canines on a leash. They were large, intimidating brown dogs.

"Which one of you is Griff and which one of you is Gladys?" the lead officer asked.

"I'm Gladys. That heartsick fool over there is Griff," Gladys pointed.

Sam placed a hand on her brother's arm and turned him back to the group. Seeing the police, he took a deep breath and shook hands, introducing himself.

"What can I do to help?"

"Gladys, take us to the scene. Everyone else, please, just let us do our job. We know you are worried. We know you want to help. Someone will have seen the van and we will find them."

"Officer, no offense, but we aren't sitting this one out. At least let us drive around and see if we spot the van. The more eyes out there the sooner we get Piper back," Griff spoke with calm authority.

Whether it was the determination in his stance or the fact that the police preferred not to tangle with the son of the mayor, who knows. The officer nodded.

"Do not try to apprehend the suspect," he warned.

Sam, Griffin, and Gladys nodded in agreement.

Pastor Dan spoke up. "Let's pray," he said as he held his hands out.

The four joined hands and hearts as Pastor Dan prayed for the safety of both Piper and the search group, and success in finding Piper soon.

"I'll stay here and relay information," Pastor Dan offered.

With a call of thanks over their shoulders, the friends hurried to Griff's truck.

SIXTEEN

I woke up with my head pounding. There was an itch too, like something was on my forehead. I wanted to scratch it but found that was impossible. Now, fully conscious, I became painfully aware that my hands were tied above my head on some sort of pipe. I was dangling but could feel the floor under my knees.

I searched my hazy memory for how I ended up here. That's right, the fire. I saw someone who didn't belong in the crowd.

Abigail. I thought back to the moment I caught up with Abigail in the parking lot outside of the spa.

~

"Hey Abigail," I tapped her on the shoulder as she was trying to push through the last of the people, towards all of the cars in the parking lot.

"Oh! Hi, Piper. Sorry, I didn't see you there," Abby said while she continued to ease away from me. Odd. I was fairly certain she looked straight at me when I caught a glimpse of her.

"That's okay. Is Deidra here today?" I asked. It was a weekday which meant Abigail would be working, so I was reaching for the only explanation that made sense for her to be here.

"Um, no. No, it's just me. I had to make some arrangements."

"I see. Is she planning a big party or something? I saw you in the garden the other day, as well, but Sam hasn't mentioned anything coming up."

Abigail shook her head hard back and forth, taking a few more steps back. I followed, thinking it was still kind of noisy and maybe she was not comfortable in big crowds. "I wasn't here. I haven't been here all week. You must be mistaken."

"I'm certain I saw you…" As Abby wiped her palms on the side of her slacks and straightened her jacket, I saw the movement loosened a folded paper in her pocket. The paper was now edging dangerously close to falling out.

"I said you didn't see me," Abby snapped and the paper fluttered to the ground, open. I bent to pick it up, shocked, barely able to process what I was seeing. Abby's eyes widened as I stood and looked at her, really looked at her. Shorter, blonde. Keeps appearing at the spa but swears she hasn't been here. My brain chugged slowly to a conclusion at the same time that Abby's face transformed into a dark, hateful scowl. She took off running into the parking lot and I dashed after her, determined to have answers.

Too bad for me, she was waiting. I rounded the corner of a large van and Abigail swung the door open, hitting me so hard I fell to the ground. My head bumped the van as I fell, white spots appeared in my vision before they, and everything else, faded to black.

~

I shook off the memory, then stopped as pain rushed through my head. There was tape over my mouth and tape around my ankles, binding them together. An empty roll of duct-tape lay nearby. That explained why a heavy scarf was on my wrists, Abigail must not have brought enough duct-tape. Typically, I hated it when people weren't prepared but, in this case, I was extremely grateful; surely the knots in a scarf would be easier to work out than removing the duct tape.

Before I could get started with my escape attempt a door swung open. Abigail climbed into the back of the van, joining me. The door slammed shut behind her; I glimpsed sunlight and dunes. Abigail must have driven me to a deserted section of beach. Not good.

~

"Piper, Piper, Piper," she clucked and shook her head in a show of disappointment. "Why did you try to ruin everything?"

"Whatrtkinbt," I screamed furiously through the duct-tape, not caring if she understood or not. I didn't understand what this crazy woman thought I ruined but I had to find a way to get far from her and soon.

"I just popped in to say hello and make sure you were still alive. That's quite the nasty little bump you have on your head," Abigail taunted, thumping me on the head.

I scowled, growling and lunging toward her. My efforts failed, my tied wrists dragging along the pole and wrenching me to a stop.

"Nuh-uh-uh," she wagged a finger at me. "Pathetic, as always. Why you ever thought you had a chance with Griffin is beyond me. As if he would ever be interested in someone who looks like a kindergartener colored their hair with a crayon. You play with cookies for a living, for goodness sake! He needs someone polished and beautiful. Someone socially adept to run his home when he is the mayor. Someone like me." She beamed.

It took a minute for my pounding head to catch up with her ramblings. The pieces slid slowly into place. The notes, ruining my dress, the rumors about Griffin getting married. This had nothing to do with the contest or trafficking rings. Abigail had lost her mind. This delusional woman had created her own little fantasy life with Griff. And somehow, in the crazy town that was her mind, I was a threat to that fictional life. Well, that would teach me to give her free cookies at my bakery.

"Now, fortunately for you I have an appointment with Deidra, can't keep the future mommy-in-law waiting you know, but I'll be back to deal with you soon."

With a slap to my cheek, Abigail turned and got out of the back of the van as quickly as she entered. The door banged shut and the horn beeped.

I was locked in.

I took a huge breath through my nose. I couldn't panic. That wouldn't do any good, I watched too many crime shows on television to panic. The calm, rational victims were always more likely to escape.

I hoped.

SEVENTEEN

So, what did we have? It was dark back here, no windows, so I could assume a delivery van of some sort. From my glimpse out of the back door, I had already surmised Abigail parked the van on a remote beach or in the dunes of one. I had no idea how long I had been unconscious but, judging by the amount of sunlight, it wasn't too late in the afternoon yet.

Of course, internally I argued with myself over whether that was good or not. If it had been less than an hour since I was taken, nobody might realize I was missing yet, especially with all of the chaos going on with the fire department at the spa.

Then again, I also thought, not being missing long was also a positive. It meant I was in no danger of starvation or needing to use the bathroom.

Yet.

Okay, Piper, I told myself, *don't think about using the bathroom, or the lapping of the waves that were probably right outside, or how thirsty duct-tape makes you.* Great. Now I need to pee.

Or perhaps the sunlight wasn't an indication of anything, my inner worrier voice screamed; maybe I had already been missing a whole day. How could nobody look for me for a whole day? No. I wouldn't think like that. I couldn't have been unconscious over twenty-four hours; I would just believe I hadn't been missing long and hope that soon someone came looking for me.

In the meantime, I continued surveying what little of my surroundings I could see as my eyes readjusted to the darkness. Thin cracks of light spilled in around the edges of the doors. Thank God for small miracles. It looked like there were a few folded tables and tablecloths back here but nothing useful that I could see. This seemed to be a large, event van and I guessed the pipe I was tied to was a garment rack of some sort.

If my head weren't pounding so much it would be a lot easier to think straight. I tried standing on my tip-toes to push my head up higher. After three attempts I was wobbling but successful. The duct-tape was tight enough to make my ankles grind against each other, I felt tears sting my eyes. Gritting my teeth, I strained toward my bound hands. Even though I was very close to reaching them, the way my wrists and fingers were tied pointing straight up above the pipe made it impossible for me to work them into removing the duct tape from my mouth. There went plan A; I had hoped to pull off the duct tape and chew the knots of the scarf loose.

Looks like it's time for plan B.

Now, what exactly would I do for plan B?

I wonder how far this pipe goes. I crouched low and hopped my bound feet forward, stumbling repeatedly but never falling down thanks to the pipe yanking my arms and keeping me upright every time. Every muscle and tendon screamed. My fingers were numbing one by one thanks to a loss of circulation. My experiment worked though. Painful hop after painful hop, I made it all the way down to the end of the pipe and was pleased to find it ran the length of the van, all the way to the back doors. My mind whirring with this information, I formulated a new plan.

~

Dozing on and off, wiggling my fingers over and over in a desperate attempt to keep any sort of circulation moving through them, I waited. It seemed an eternity but at last, I heard the click of the doors unlocking. I roused myself, scooting as close to the door as possible. The door swung open and I poured all of my energy into an awkward hop-kick, slamming my bound feet into Abigail's chest as she made to step into the back of the van. She fell backward, the open door revealing it was almost dusk. I hopped like mad, yelled through the duct-tape, even slammed my feet into the wall over and over again to make as much noise as physically possible in my position.

Abigail was barely dazed. The sand softened her landing and much too soon she was angrily grasping the door, pulling herself up. I tried to kick out again but she was ready for me this time. Catching my legs, she shoved me out of the way and slammed the door. Abigail turned on the flashlight app of her phone and shone the bright light in my eyes. I blinked, turning my head away.

"That was pretty stupid, Piper. You don't think anybody can hear you, do you?" she asked as she sat the phone down in a corner, lighting up most of the space. "Ugh! Look, you've ruined my outfit," she flailed her hands against her clothes as she tried to get all of the dirt and grit off of her white slacks. Great. Not only had I been kidnapped by a crazy woman but, at this rate, she was probably the type to leave me hanging here even longer while she ran to the dry cleaners. Funny, just a few days ago I had been feeling sorry for her as Deidra's assistant. Now, I was wishing she had choked on a pastry.

Giving up on her precious suit, Abigail glared back at me.

"Come on, I'm ready to get rid of you and be finished with this. Then I can get Griffin to propose to me and never think about this messy business again."

Lunatic. Wait. Get rid of me? I darted a glance at her hands. No gun. No purse to hold a gun in that I could see. Maybe I still had time to get away.

She narrowed her eyes and regarded me warily.

"Listen. This would be much easier if you could walk yourself to the pier from which you will tragically fall to your death but if you try anything, I will knock you out and drag you there myself. Do you understand?"

I nodded, completely agreeing with her; it would be much easier if I could walk.

Abigail unbound my wrists from the pole but relief was not to come. Yanking my arms behind my back she re-tied the scarf, the fabric biting into my skin. I'd be burning all my scarves after this adventure, provided I ever saw my scarves again. Sharp, needle-like sensations ran through my hands as the blood began flowing down into them again. Steering me from behind, she made me hop to the back door.

"Sit down," she instructed and I did.

Opening the door of the van just a crack to check for any people, Abigail must have determined the coast to be clear. She stepped outside and shut the door. I had a moment of panic; I thought she was letting me out to walk somewhere. *Where did she go? Did she decide to drive the van into the ocean instead,* I wondered as I heard a door at the front of the van open and shut. But no. The back door opened again.

"Forgot my scissors up front," she said as she pulled off my shoes and then cut the duct tape from my ankles. I rolled my eyes. I never knew it could be so frustrating to be kidnapped by an exceptionally unprepared person; she had nearly given me a heart attack thinking I was going to drown in this van.

"Out," Abigail ordered. Grabbing me by the elbow, she pointed me down the beach and we started walking. I drank in the sight of my surroundings, praying for someone or something familiar. Abigail had mentioned a pier.

There weren't many piers in Seashell Bay that wouldn't be full of people. I could think of only two piers in remote locations near here. One was the pier in the next town that had been mostly torn apart in a recent storm and was labeled condemned, roped off to be torn down when the city got around to it. The other was equally as dangerous. They called it Pirate Pier. Pirate Pier was probably only twenty minutes from the spa, but it was too far away from the nightlife and carnival piers to attract tourists. It had been unofficially claimed by the local druggies; deals went down there and anyone unfortunate enough to stumble across them accidentally usually left with their wallet much lighter. The cops stopped checking it out months ago because no matter the tip, someone, either a lookout or a dirty cop, warned off the dealers before they arrived.

Pain sliced through my foot and I crumpled to one knee, my elbow slipping from Abigail's grasp before she knew it. Broken glass bottles and garbage littered the area. Blood oozed from a cut in my heel. My guess, we were close to Pirate Pier and there would either be nobody there to help me, or simply nobody who cared to make it their business.

"Get up," Abigail's hushed voice broke into my thoughts. She dragged me to my feet and we continued forward. Sand burned as it ground into the cut on my heel and I played up my limp to stall for more time. It was well past twilight now, the moon glinted off of the ocean to our left. In the distance, if I squinted, I could just make out shapes jutting from the water. We were nearly there.

Muffled sounds came from behind us and then shouts could be distinguished. People! I jerked to a halt and yelled, muffled by tape that it was, as loud as possible.

"Shut up, shut up!" Abigail's harsh whisper tickled my ear. She pushed me forward but my determination was renewed.

I heard Samantha and then Griff. I heard dogs barking. This was it, someone was coming to save me. Flashlights bounced around as I continued to make noise. Abigail flew into a panic and tried to drag me when I wouldn't budge but she stumbled and we both crashed to the ground.

I rolled away from Abigail and in the precious moments of her confusion, I was able to scrape the duct-tape off of my mouth with my knee. It took a lot of spitting and slobbering to loosen it up but I was willing to try anything.

The moment it came partway loose I began shouting as loud as my lungs could manage.

"Help! Sam, Griff, help!" Flashlights shot our direction. I could hear the dogs and a few footsteps getting closer. Abigail kicked me, striking a glancing blow to my leg as I yelled and rolled. The scarf on my wrists caught on a piece of driftwood. I yanked and nearly cried in relief when I heard a small tear. I pulled and rubbed and pulled, not even sure it would work but finally, the scarf tore and my battered wrists fell free. The lights were nearly to us. I could see Abigail groping in the dirt. When she stood up, my heart nearly stopped; she had found a half-broken bottle and was coming right at me with no regard to the rescuers coming closer.

"You. You can't have him. If I can't have him, you can't have him." She was screaming at me now, only three steps away. I jumped up, fumbling my hand into the side of my bra under my arm at the same time. I dug my feet into the sand, gripping with my toes like my life depended on it; my ankles were still bound and keeping my balance was so hard. Finally, I pulled my pocket knife free of my bra just as Abigail raised the bottle above her head. Fumbling to make use of my nearly dead hands, I flipped the knife open and thrust it toward her just as she lunged. The bottle missed my head and cut a jagged line down my shoulder. Time seemed to slow down. I let go of the knife and stepped back, tripping over the driftwood that freed me; Abigail's body fell with a thud in the sand right next to me. I shrank back, unable to look at her. I didn't want to know if I had killed her or not.

Hands caught my shoulders and I screamed and flailed my arms at them. Griff's voice penetrated the shock ever so slowly. "Piper, it's okay. I've got you."

Sam threw herself into the dirt on my other side. This was a woman who didn't care about ruined clothing, I thought to myself in a distracted way. I could hear her and Griff, but their voices were fuzzy almost like they came from far away. The sheriff caught my eye next, as he bent down and cut the tape from my ankles. Griff stepped away to talk to the sheriff, I caught the words hospital and tomorrow. Sam hugged me close.

~

By nine the next morning, I was cranky, hungry, and ready to go home. The nurse insisted I had to wait until the doctor made one more round before I could be released from the hospital. Sam agreed with her, the traitor. A soft knock on the door announced the arrival of another visitor. Gladys peeked around the door.

"May I come in?"

I waved her forward, a small gesture, moving my body as little as possible. I didn't dare to risk nodding since my head felt like a stampeding herd of horses had taken up residence there. Gladys came and stood by the bed.

"Your nails still look great," she pointed to my toes which had survived the barefoot trek unscathed. Leave it to Gladys to find the positive side of something.

"Thanks," I said sarcastically.

"Here, I brought you something," she said, opening up her large neon orange purse. Why neon orange I have no idea since it clashed completely with her pink velour tracksuit. I didn't care though when I saw what she brought; in fact, I was prepared to kiss that neon orange purse. Out of it Gladys pulled an entire bag of dark chocolate chips and passed them to me.

Sam smiled. "Well, Gladys, Piper is just in heaven now."

I accepted the bag of chocolate chips with a grin.

"Thanks, Gladys, and have I told you yet how sorry I was that we suspected you?"

"Don't worry about all that. I'm glad you are okay."

I tossed a palm full of dark chocolate into my mouth and closed my eyes, savoring the rich and bitter notes as I let it slowly dissolve over my tongue.

"Now," I swallowed and looked at them both. "I've told you everything that happened to me. I want to know what was going on at the spa and everything that led you to find me. I never did hear what the fire department found when they showed up."

EIGHTEEN

"You go ahead," Gladys told Sam.

"Alright, here goes," Sam began. "I went to talk to Rick, one of the firemen, and Pastor Dan to see what was happening. It turns out there was no fire. All of that smoke we saw, that was because five smoke bombs were set off in the yoga studio and one of the windows broken. The smoke was more than enough to set off the smoke detectors. The sprinkler system evidently malfunctioned and never went off so, in a way, it was a blessing that the smoke bombs made the spa aware of the issue in time to fix it before a real fire happens."

"Who set off the smoke bombs? And why?" I asked.

"We weren't sure for a while, but we think now that it was Abigail. We can't confirm it, or her motives, but Felicity says she was in the hallway when a woman with short, blonde hair ducked past her in quite the hurry. Whether Abigail was trying to cause a distraction to hurt you or to get into your room and do something else I have no idea. She isn't talking, not even to confess to the smoke bombs."

"So, so I didn't kill her?" I asked looking up at Sam.

"No don't worry, she isn't dead. She has a pretty nasty wound in her side but she lived. The sheriff is working to get her transferred to a prison hospital far from here as soon as possible and to make sure she never gets out to hurt anyone again. There were enough witnesses on the beach that nobody thinks the prosecution will be difficult."

I nodded, still numb. I supposed I was glad I hadn't killed someone but at the same time, I didn't feel the relief I expected that news to bring.

"Tell her how you found her," Gladys leaned forward, prodding Sam to continue telling me what all had happened in the search for me.

Sam took a breath and launched into the telling.

"While I was still with Pastor Dan, Griff showed up looking for you. He was babbling about some woman trying to get Mother to arrange a marriage between the two of them, how she kept calling him and saying they were meant to be and that he had to find you and make sure you knew it wasn't true. I thought he was out of his mind because he kept asking if you were mad about the dress, he wasn't making any sense. When we were searching for the van I finally got him to slow down and talk to me. He explained that he had sent you the silver dress as a gift because of your phone call worrying about clothes and the text about the ruined dress the other night. I asked why in the world he didn't include a note and he said there was a card attached. That is when I remembered what Jill said about the blonde knocking into her in the hall and the card being gone. It all started to fit together, in an insane kind of way. I told him that I thought a blonde woman took the card."

Sam paused and stole a drink from my water cup. "Remind me to get you some tea," she said then leaped back into the story. "Right about then Gladys came running up."

"Or as close to running as someone my age gets," Gladys interjected.

"She told us some blonde put you in a van. Griff called 911 to get people to help find you; Gladys took a photo of the license plate so I texted it to myself and posted it as an emergency on Facebook. By the time Gladys showed Griff where Abigail took you, the van was gone. It had no identifying logos on the outside but thanks to that license plate, we had a good start."

"Gladys, thank you! Thank you so much, I don't know what I would have done if you hadn't got that plate number and the search party hadn't found me."

"I just wish I could have stopped her. But I didn't know how dangerous she was and I'm not all that strong; I knew I couldn't do anything by myself so I took the picture and got help as fast as I could. It was a miracle I even saw you, really. I was tired of getting bumped into in the crowd so I was trying to find a bench to sit down on out by the parking area. When I saw her shoving you in the van I froze. Thankfully, I ducked behind a palm tree and the crazy lady didn't see me taking the photo as she drove away."

I had a moment of wondering if Gladys spoke to the palm trees while she took the photos of me being abducted and nearly laughed. Maybe I was delirious from pain meds. I kept my face straight though and listened as they continued.

"Well after we called 911 and they showed up to coordinate the search," Sam picked up, "I had posted the license plate photo on Facebook, like I said, with an emergency help request. Everybody's on the thing twenty-four-seven, I figured we might as well use it. Thankfully a few sightings led the police to predict the route Abigail was taking would lead to the beach. We started the search at the nearest beach access to the last van sighting. The dogs were given your scent and the scent from the area where the van had parked. We had no luck during the first two hours so the police decided to try some of the more remote access points. At the last one, only one set of vehicle tracks were in the sand, and they were pretty fresh. We found the van soon after and let the dogs take it from there."

"I'd like to kiss those dogs," I said.

"We could finally see you lying on the ground and it looked like Abigail was getting ready to hit you with something. Griff took off running like he was back on the track team, the sheriff right on his heels yelling at him to stay back. Everything happened fast and by the time I got to you, well, Abigail wasn't a threat anymore. The sheriff kept insisting he needed to get your statement but Griff refused to allow it, saying you needed rest and a doctor and food before anything else. I think he may have threatened to call Dad if the sheriff bothered you before nine this morning."

"Griffin was beside himself thinking he was somehow responsible for getting you hurt. That poor boy wouldn't even eat the cookies I offered him after we had been searching for hours," Gladys shook her head sadly.

"Why would Griff think it was his fault?" I wondered aloud.

"Because it kind of was," a gruff voice spoke from the doorway and we all turned. Griffin stood there, disheveled, with sand clinging to some of his clothes, dark stubble covering his normally clean-shaven face.

"Griffin!" Sam stood and dusted off some of her brother's clothes. "Did you not go home to shower and sleep?"

"Couldn't sleep."

"Sam, why don't you and I step out and find that tea for Piper?" Gladys nodded toward the hospital corridor.

"Fine. Piper, we will be right back," she assured me.

"Griffin, you can come in," I told him when he made no move past the door frame.

"Piper, I'm so sorry. How are you doing?" he asked pulling a chair closer to the bed.

"I'm fine. Truly. Just some scrapes and a couple of stitches on my head. The doctor said I didn't even sustain a concussion." I rubbed my wrists self-consciously, hoping the dark and ugly bruising would disappear as fast as my paychecks usually did.

"That's great to hear. I can't believe Abigail took you. I've never been so scared in my life."

"Thanks, Griff." Warmth that had nothing to do with the hospital blankets stole up my neck and I hoped he didn't notice the blush. "Maybe you can fill in some blanks for me though. Starting with why in the world you think any of this is your fault."

A nurse came in to check some things on the machine next to my bed and Griffin shifted uncomfortably in the chair until she left.

Clearing his throat, he said, "Abigail has always been very friendly to me, maybe overly-friendly, but I thought it was because she assisted Mother. I had no idea she was so delusional or I never would have asked her advice. You see, after that incredibly cute phone call when you were flipping out over what to wear to the spa…"

"I was not flipping out," I crossed my arms over my stomach.

"Yeah, okay," he smirked. "Well, after that I wanted to get you a present that would make you more excited about your wardrobe. I got Gladys to go through your clothes to find out your size after you got to the spa. And then you sounded so sad in your text about how your dress had been messed up, so I thought a new dress would be perfect."

"Wait! Do you mean that Gladys was in my room that day when she denied it? Why didn't you ask Sam?"

"Please, give me some credit. I know my sister and she doesn't keep any secrets from you. There was no way I was letting her ruin my surprise."

To be fair, that made complete sense. I nodded, then winced as I received a kick from one of the many ponies prancing on my brain.

"Are you sure you're okay?" Griff asked.

"Yes."

"Anyway, after Gladys got the information for me on your size, I asked Abigail where a nice place to buy a dress was. Being Mother's assistant, I knew she would have all of the information on what stores would be the best places to shop. I wanted the dress to be perfect. I didn't know that by asking her I would be pushing her crazy button and setting her on some jealous rampage."

"That doesn't make sense," I rubbed my forehead. "The first note I received was at the bakery before I called Sam about what to pack."

"Yes, Sam told me about the notes. When I asked her about places to buy the type of dress I wanted, she told me it was heartless of me to get your hopes up by flirting with you in the bakery and then buying you gifts. She said that my mother would never approve of you and that I should set my sights on someone more worthwhile. She must have already been angry about hearing me talk to you at the bakery a few days before. When I asked about the dress, it was like rubbing salt in a wound that I didn't know existed." Griff rubbed his palms down his face and sighed. "I made it abundantly clear that who I did or did not have a relationship with was neither my mother's business nor her business and then I left without a store recommendation. I think that was enough to send her into some kind of spiral and unleash her jealous rage on you and for that, I am so sorry."

"Griff, you could never have guessed she would react violently. You've never led her on. Why didn't you just tell Abigail that you and I were friends?"

Griffin reached for my hand. "Piper, I don't think…" He was interrupted by an abrupt rap on the door.

Sheriff Kent stepped inside. "Good morning, Miss Rivers. I need to take your statement. This young man convinced me to let you rest last night, but I really have to get it from you now."

"Of course, Sheriff. I understand," I told him. "Thank you for waiting."

Griff squeezed my hand. "We'll talk later, Piper." Shaking hands with the sheriff, Griff excused himself and left. I hoped he was going home to rest and shower; he looked in worse shape than I felt.

Sheriff Kent opted to stand when I invited him to sit.

"Won't take but a minute," he insisted.

I took a drink from my water glass, wondering where Sam and Gladys were with that tea, and then started at the beginning with the note at the bakery.

~

"You saw Miss Abigail Fletcher was about to strike you with the broken bottle we found. Where did the weapon come from that she was stabbed with? Did you take it from her?"

Sam and Gladys had returned in the course of the sheriff's questions, remaining quietly at the door so as not to interrupt. Sam had to cover her chuckle and walk away when I answered this last one.

"No, sir. The pocket knife is, was, my own. My father gave me my first knife when I was twelve to keep for self-defense. I've carried one so long I quit thinking of it as a weapon and merely as a tool that was always on hand. I got into the habit of never being without one. The knife was clipped to the side of my bra because I didn't have any pockets yesterday, there was nowhere else to put it. I couldn't reach it when Abigail held me in the van but I finally got my hands free and grabbed it on the beach. I hope I never have to use one like that again." I shivered. "But I think I should call Dad and tell him thank you."

"No need to call," Sam piped up. "Your parents are on their way here. Their flight lands in about two hours."

Tears flooded my eyes. My friend, always determined to take care of me. "I don't know what I would do without you," I told her gratefully.

"Probably sit home and eat chocolate," she told me in her matter-of-fact way.

"Okay, Miss Rivers," the sheriff said as he closed his steno pad, "I think I have everything I need from you. You take care."

The second the sheriff disappeared from the room, Sam burst out, "Piper! Did I hear you tell the sheriff you had a knife in your bra?"

"Yes. I had no pockets, where do you expect me to keep it? The summer after Landon was taken, my dad gave me a pocket knife and taught me some of the basics of self-defense. I'll admit I let my lessons lapse and probably couldn't tell you the difference between carrot and karate, but the habit of carrying some type of weapon never left."

"Smart girl," Gladys commented.

Sam, Gladys and I drank our tea and passed around the bag of dark chocolate chips until it was time for Sam to pick up my parents at the airport.

"By the way," she said as she fished in her purse looking for her keys, "my mother is angry with you."

I closed my eyes and leaned back into the pillows. "Your mother has never liked me, Sam. Why is today any different?"

"She says you cost her a perfectly good secretary and wants to know why they will not release Abigail after, and I quote 'the little cat fight over my son'."

"You have got to be kidding me."

"Nope. You know Deidra, puts whatever spin she wants to on things. It has inconvenienced her so someone must be to blame. Lucky you, she can just add it to the list of ways you are destroying her perfect life."

"Fine. Whatever." It didn't matter if it was ludicrous; Deidra Lowe was resolute when she made up her mind to something.

Keys in hand, Sam bent to give me a hug. "Back in a few," she said to me. Then to Gladys, "Keep an eye on her okay?"

Gladys gave Sam a thumbs up. "You bet."

It didn't seem like very long at all before Sam was back with Mom and Dad.

"Oh! Piper, my goodness we would have come to visit without all this drama if you had called and invited us," Mom joked with a twinkle in her eye as she hugged me tightly.

Dad, of course, brought his own bag and was steadily unpacking a stethoscope and pulling out the light to check my eyes for pupil constriction.

"No," I told him.

"Honey, I just want to see…"

"No, Dad. I'm fine. Put it away."

"But…"

"Nope," I folded my arms across my chest. Mom slapped at his hand. Mumbling he repacked his doctor bag and moved it to the floor.

"We can't tell you how happy we are you are okay," Dad told me as he kissed my forehead like he had been doing since I was a little kid. "Can we get you anything?"

My stomach growled. "Yes. Lunch. Go find someone who can release me. Stat." I smiled.

"On it," Dad grinned and I knew I would be out in minutes.

"I'm going to make sure he doesn't make anyone cry," my mom chuckled, following him from the room. My heart filled at the sight of the love the two still shared.

We decided to order pizza and eat at my apartment; I hadn't showered yet and was not ready to go out in public. Gladys offered to drive me and my parents to my apartment while Sam picked up the pizza. Sam left first and Gladys followed to pull her car around to the front of the hospital. I leaned my head back again. I hated to admit how tired I really felt.

The sound of the door opening was a relief. "It's about time. It took you a whole three minutes to get me released Dad," I taunted, smirking just a little.

"It is about time, Piper; how right you are," a wheezy voice rasped.

I sat straight up, heart racing. Abigail, with an IV drip and some type of monitor handcuffed to her wrist, leaned against the door frame. After she caught her breath, she half-walked and half-leaned on the rolling machine, coming towards my bed.

NINETEEN

I couldn't believe it.

Would this nightmare never end?

Abigail bumped into the end of the bed, jostling my bag of chocolate chips from their hiding place. As they scattered across the room, my fear fled as well. I was fed up with this crazy woman.

"Are you kidding me?" I screamed at her. "That is the last time you ruin my chocolate." I chunked the tv remote at her head.

She ducked, losing her balance and the machine tilted. I kept throwing things. Pillows, magazines, finally I tossed my water cup at her. The liquid sloshed in a puddle at her feet and Abigail finally went down, hitting the footboard on her way. The machine crashed onto her head and she lay still. I watched in horror as blood slowly soaked through her hospital gown, her stab wound having been reopened.

I considered getting up to check on her but decided against it. No way I wanted to be close to her again. Dad entered the room at that moment, all smiles, trailed by Mom and my attending nurse. The nurse saw the crumpled woman on my floor and yelled into the hallway for help. Dad for once stood flabbergasted but Mom practically vaulted the mess on the floor, stepping in the visitor chair and over the nurse, to get to my side.

The nurse looked up at us, removing her fingers from Abigail's wrist. "She's…dead."

It turns out, Abigail's neck had been broken, snapped on the footboard during the fall and killing her instantly.

A blur of activity followed.

Dad sprinted from the room to catch up with the sheriff whom he had seen at the nurse's station on the floor below while having me released.

The sheriff, of course, had to come and take more statements from me. "Well, Miss Rivers. It looks like we won't have to worry about a trial after all. Clearly, this death was accidental and in self-defense. I may have a few more questions when I finish up the paperwork but for now, I hope you can begin to recover and find some peace."

By the time we arrived at my apartment, Sam had been waiting for about fifteen minutes. Giving her a giant hug, I went straight to the shower without speaking, leaving my parents to explain everything that had happened after she left the hospital.

I showered and dressed in the softest sweater I owned and some thick cotton pajama pants, feeling almost human again. My wrists were still pretty sore but I felt like they would heal quickly.

The tough part would be erasing the gory images of Abigail's body being removed from the hospital floor and zipped into a black body bag.

When I joined everyone in the living room, Gladys was there as well. She had come over to check on if I was settling in ok. Sam and my parents insisted she stay for pizza. She had, after all, been crucial in finding me. Dad also insisted on checking my pupils but didn't push any further than that. They asked if I was up to talking about why Abigail was so determined to hurt me and so I filled in all the details of Abigail's delusions and my stalker notes at the spa for Mom and Dad as we ate.

"Thanks, Dad," I told him when I finished. "If it hadn't been for you insisting that I carry that knife years ago who knows if I would have made it off of that beach last night."

"You are tough," Mom said. "You would have found a way. I'm so glad Samantha's brother and the sheriff got there so quickly yesterday. I'm so sorry we left you alone in the hospital room today for that, that psycho to try again."

"Tell me about this Griffin though," Dad said as he crossed his arms. "Is there something we should know? This Abigail woman seemed pretty convinced you were standing between her and her fairytale prince."

I rolled my eyes. "Griffin is Sam's brother, Dad. You know that. He was looking out for me just like he looks out for his sister."

Gladys choked on her water. I shot her a dirty look behind my parents' backs; no need for Gladys to interject her own crazy theories about Griff and me here either.

Sam's phone rang, cutting off the glaring contest between me and Gladys.

"Excuse me," she said as she left the room to answer the call.

There were a few moments of quiet as we each chewed on our pizza and reflected on our own thoughts. Sam returned to the room rather quickly, placing the phone back on the side table as she plopped down on the sofa.

"Piper, that was Pastor Dan. He called to check on you and to invite us and your family to a small dinner tonight."

"That was sweet of him," I smiled.

"He feels so bad that we missed out on the last day of our spa stay and said the least they could do is hold a dinner to celebrate you being found quickly and safely. I told him what happened and that I wasn't sure if you would be up to it."

"Mom? Dad? Would you like to join us for dinner this evening on Pastor Dan's invitation?" I asked my parents.

"That would be wonderful," Mom responded for them both.

"I think we should go," I told Sam. "It will be good to get my mind off of things."

"Great," Sam said. "I'll send him a message after we finish this pizza."

My parents insisted on heading to a hotel so that I could take a nap. I'm not going to lie, a nap sounded perfect so I didn't even argue; I hugged them both and arranged for Gladys to pick them up on her way to dinner at the church that evening since the hotel was closest to her.

Sam promised to come back and pick me up later. Everyone was insistent I shouldn't overdo it and they evidently considered driving to be on the list of things that were too stressful for me right now. I supposed I should probably be annoyed or frustrated with them but all I felt was loved and blessed. I tossed the pizza boxes into the recycle bin, washed my hands and then escaped to my bedroom as the door closed behind the last of my guests.

I didn't sleep for nearly as long as I expected that I would. I managed to take around a thirty-minute nap but was wide awake after that. Perhaps it was being home after so many days away. Maybe it was relishing the feeling of being alive and free and safe. Whatever it was, I felt like it would be a shame to waste another second in bed.

I got up and tidied my little apartment. I noticed my duffle tucked beside the couch; Sam or Gladys must have brought it home for me. The thought made me smile and I picked it up, carrying it to the laundry nook where I began to separate lights and darks. The ruined white dress wasn't a part of the contents for which I was happy. I don't care if someone threw it away, I definitely had no plans to salvage and wear it again. My beautiful new silver dress was also missing. A pang shot through my chest; I was saddened that I hadn't even worn it yet. Maybe I could ask the staff tonight after dinner if someone had found it.

Once I had the first load of clothes started my energy began to fade but I had the perfect solution for that. Cookies!

There was a new bar cookie idea that had been tapping at the back of my head recently; today, I would try it out. I stood on tiptoe, stretching to reach the large blue mixing bowl on the second shelf of my cabinet. The other supplies I gathered from various places in the kitchen. For the ingredients, I grabbed flour, butter, eggs, brown sugar, cream of tartar, baking soda, hazelnut extract, dark chocolate, coconut flakes, and pecans.

I breathed in the delicious scent of melted butter and sugar with the hazelnut extract as I added the eggs and creamed it all together.

The dry ingredients were next. With each thing I put into the bowl, the stress slowly eased from my neck and my thoughts centered on the mixture right in front of me; everything else drifted away.

A bit of the dark chocolate went into the batter, the rest I sprinkled on the top of the bars in thick layers so it would melt over everything while they baked. I garnished with the pecans and coconut flakes and popped it into a three-hundred-fifty-degree oven.

Ding-dong. My doorbell rang just over an hour later. I went to open it, stopping to check the peephole for the first time in ages, obviously I was still shaken up, and smiled to see Sam on my doorstep.

"You're early," I greeted.

"Yep. And you've been baking, I can smell it."

Grinning, I led the way to the kitchen.

"Just a little something to tide us over until the dinner tonight," I told her. "Here try one, they should be plenty cool by now." I grabbed a butter knife from the drawer and cut two bars from the pan.

Sam bit into the sample I handed her and closed her eyes.

She licked her lips before declaring, "Love it!" We finished off the ooey-gooey bars and I placed two more on a plate to carry to the living room.

"I was thinking of calling them Chocoloconut Bars. I'm glad you like them."

"Are you kidding? They are scrumptious!"

"What's in the bag?" I asked pointing at the bag Sam had deposited in the door of the living room when we passed by on the way to the kitchen.

She picked up the bag and pulled out my beautiful silver dress. "This got packed up with my things. I thought you should wear it tonight."

"Thank you, I was afraid it had been lost."

"You're welcome. I brought my dress, too, so we can just get ready here."

"Perfect," I sat down gingerly on the couch and pulled up the guide on the tv. "Until then, what do you want to watch?"

Two and a half episodes of Cupcake Wars later, Sam stretched.

"Okay," she said, "let's get moving or we'll never be ready to go."

I watched with a bit of awe and a bit of apprehension as Sam pulled gadget after brush after tube out of her magic bag.

"That is way more than just a dress," I pointed out sarcastically.

"Yeah well, we missed our last spa day so for tonight we get the works. Come on, it'll be fun; like playing dress up when we were girls."

"I never played dress up."

"No time like the present," Sam retorted.

I gave in, as she knew I would. Sam plugged in a few things and laid them on the coffee table. I hit play again. If she was going to straighten or curl or who knows what to my hair right here in the living room, then I might as well be entertained. I tried to ignore the sounds of my hair sizzling.

Next, Sam sat down in front of me and spread all of the makeup products from every department store known to man on the coffee table. At least that's how many it looked like to me. "No. No to that, that and this," I said pointing to cherry red lipstick, something that looked like pink chalk dust, and what might have been a blue map pencil right away.

"Piper…" Sam pouted.

"Just use something light, no crazy club make-up. It's not like I'm going to this dinner to impress anyone."

"Okay, fine."

TWENTY

We pulled up in the dining hall parking lot, with Sam avoiding the main spa parking lot out front, and I could see Gladys and my parents waiting by the entrance. As I stepped out of the small Juke, I smoothed wrinkles from my dress with both hands. I took a deep breath, in and out, and then reached for my small clutch that held my phone and tissues and a thin wallet.

I looked up to find Sam watching me, her normally smooth face etched with soft concern, eyes sharp.

"I'm fine," I reassured her. "What's on the menu tonight anyway?"

We linked arms and made our way to the small group at the door, Pastor Dan and his wife Nora had joined the others. I was squished into a giant group hug by both of my parents the moment I stepped next to them.

"Gosh guys, you just saw me a few hours ago," I laughed to take the bite out of the words and hugged them back.

Pastor Dan was next.

"Piper, I'm so glad you and Samantha were able to make it tonight. And it is wonderful to meet your parents. Allow me to introduce my wife, this is Nora."

"Hello, Nora," I shook her hand and was pulled into another bear hug.

"Well hi, honey," Nora beamed a million-watt smile, "let's get you in here and find some food, what do you say?"

"I say, lead the way," I told the sweet woman. Pastor Dan absolutely glowed when he looked at her; they made a great match.

The dining hall was quiet this evening. I noticed a long table was set with ten places.

"Who else is coming?" I whispered to Sam as we pulled our chairs out.

"Here, let me get that for you."

I whirled at the voice so close to me, toppling in the heels Sam had insisted I borrow. I would have fallen had Griff not caught my wrist and righted me.

"Don't sneak up on people," I snapped.

Griff quirked one eyebrow at me and smirked, his demeanor back to normal. He had gone home to shower finally and his face was shaven smooth once again. He seemed lighter, happier than he had been during his visit to my hospital room.

"You look good," I blurted out. "I mean, better; you look better, cleaner." In my head, I yelled at myself *shut up, shut up, shut up Piper, just sit down and be quiet for goodness sakes.*

Griff smiled as he held my chair out and pushed it in for me as I sat down, trying to calm my rapid heartbeat. I lied and told myself it was only because he startled me as I unfolded my napkin to fan my face a bit before spreading it in my lap.

"You look good too, Piper. I'm glad to see you wore the dress" Griff murmured, breath warm against my ear, before casually hugging his sister and taking a seat on the opposite side of the table.

Some shuffling chairs caught my attention and I saw Pastor Dan stand to receive the last guests. Beside me, Sam cleared her throat.

"Remember when you asked who all was coming? Surprise…Pastor Dan invited my parents to be here also."

"Oh boy," was all I could say, especially after Sam had already told me that her mother was more upset with me than usual.

"I'm sure it will be fine," Sam spoke but we both knew she was fibbing.

Mayor Gregory Lowe and the first lady Deidra greeted the pastor and his wife, shaking hands and air kissing cheeks respectively.

Sam and I stood as her parents approached our side of the table. "That is a lovely dress, Samantha," Deidra said as she held Sam at arms-length and literally inspected her. "Red looks wonderful on you, except those horrid streaks in your hair, of course."

"Of course, Mother. Thank you for letting me know," Sam rolled her eyes as she hugged her mom and then smiled brightly at her dad. "And how are you, Dad?"

"Numbers are looking good," he said brightly. Mayor Lowe had a one-track mind. Politics. Never suspecting his daughter was simply asking about his general well-being, he launched into the latest updates from the office and pole statistics as he pulled out Sam's chair for her to be seated. Deidra skirted around me as if I had the plague and followed her husband to the other side of Sam.

I looked up and saw that Griff had witnessed the snub. His brow creased and a scowl flashed across his face before he schooled his features. He caught my glance and I rolled my eyes, tilting my own nose in the air as I resumed my seat with an exaggerated air of snobbishness. I smiled and winked, letting Griff know I'm not hurt by his mother's actions. I have to look away, unnerved and a little breathless, as he smiled and continued to hold my eyes.

Thank goodness, I spotted the servers bringing out plates of food and sigh in relief. Noticing, Sam gave me an odd look.

"Hungry," I told her, not caring if she believed me.

"Pardon me, friends," Pastor Dan cleared his throat, standing up at the head of the table on my right. "I want to take a moment to thank Samantha and Piper again for the hard work and creativity they put forth to raise money for Breaking Chains. For those who aren't aware, the Ooey-Gooey-Goodness Bakery raised over $8,300 for this mission. A true blessing. And now if you will bow your heads, I will ask the blessing over our beautiful meal this evening."

Bowing my head, I let the pastor's prayer flow over me, calming me truly for the first time that evening. "Our heavenly Father," he began, "we thank you for Samantha and Piper and each of the amazing businesses in our community who gave of their hearts and their profits to help others in need. Father God, we thank you for your protection over Piper this week and ask that you heal and comfort her as the days continue. Heavenly Father, we ask that each dollar donated to this mission will be used according to your divine will to bring the most relief and help to free and prevent victims of human trafficking. You love each of those people as you love us, please help them to see and to know that. Thank you for allowing us this delicious meal and the company of friends and family. We ask that you use it to increase our health and strength that we may continue to share your love with others. It is in your son Jesus's name we pray. Amen."

A chorus of "amen" echoed Pastor Dan as he sat again at the table. "Dig in!"

You don't have to tell me twice. Garlic grilled pork chops. Yum. Crispy, seasoned sweet potato fries. Delish. Fried green beans. Finger-licking good. Cheesy Grits. Yes, please. My plate was loaded with one of everything and two of a few.

"It's been ages since I've had fried green beans," I told Sam as I popped another one in my mouth, relishing the satisfying crunch.

"Me too," Sam agreed. "Probably in Seville during college was the last time, on one of our TGI Friday nights."

I think there was also a nice healthy salad somewhere on the table but I was avoiding it.

"Oh no."

"What," Sam asked, eyes widening in alarm and whipping her head around to see what had caught my sight.

"There is dessert," I moaned. "I already ate so much food and now they bring dessert. I'm going to have to sleep under the table, no way I'll be able to walk out of here after all this food."

Sam rolled her eyes and slapped me on the shoulder. "Don't do that. You made me think Abigail came back from the dead or something. It's just dessert, suck it up or don't eat it."

"Are we even friends? Why would you suggest something monstrous like not eating dessert?" I inched my chair away from Sam, fighting back my grin.

"Lunatic," she muttered under her breath as she speared her last bite of pork chop on the end of her fork and my grin split wide open.

As the server sat the dessert in front of Pastor Dan, I nonchalantly wiped the drool off of my bottom lip. Okay. Not really. But it looked so delicious that drool was a dangerous possibility, I promise. The aroma of rich chocolate assailed my nose. All thoughts of being full vanished as I stared at the four-tier chocolate cake like a lion staring at a gazelle.

Pastor Dan handed the cutting knife to Nora, "Would you do the honors, my dear?"

Nora sliced a generous portion of cake and sat it on a small white plate, a stack of which the server had left. Pastor Dan added a clean fork to the plate and passed it down the table. I whimpered, just a little, when Sam took it from me and kept passing it down to the end. *She and I really needed to talk about this politeness thing,* I decided, *she might be taking it too far.*

Gladys declined her slice of cake. Rubbing her belly, she excused herself.

"I'm afraid I overdid it. If nobody minds, I think I'm going to go on home to bed."

"Go ahead, Gladys. I can take Piper's parents back to their hotel when we finish up here," Sam insisted.

Finally, I received a slice of cake that Sam didn't whisk away from me. Each of the four layers was separated by a chocolate and a vanilla buttercream frosting. Chocolate chips were sprinkled throughout the cake like hidden gems inside a mountain. The chocolate curls decorating the top of the cake held their shape better than my hair. It was a masterpiece.

Talk turned to pleasant subjects during dessert. Pastor Dan and Nora were curious about my parents.

"Where did you say you live Robert?" he asked my father.

"Our home is in Jenner Falls, Alabama now. However, we have been traveling across the Western side of the states for the past three months, early retirement or sabbatical – whatever you want to call it, and so California is where we flew in from when Sam called us about Piper being in the hospital."

"I've always wanted to see the Redwood National Forest," Nora spoke with a smile. "Has that been a part of your trip?"

"Yes, it is breathtaking," Mom said. "We even got in the long line of tourists to drive through the tree where you can get your picture made. Here, I probably have it on my phone somewhere."

Seeing his opening while Pastor Dan and Nora were engaged, my dad latched onto Griff's shoulder and began grilling him.

I slid lower in my seat as my stomach churned; I knew it was inevitable but I had hoped Dad would forget about the rumors of Griff and me for just a little while. Even chocolate cake couldn't make this type of embarrassment disappear.

"Tell me, Greg was it, do you have a job?"

"It's Griffin, sir. I have a career I enjoy immensely yes."

"Do you plan to tell me about it or should I guess?"

Oh gosh. My face bloomed scarlet and my temper built like a shaken coke bottle.

"Dad stop it!" I hissed across the table.

"Now Piper, don't be upset. I can't get to know the man if I don't ask questions, now can I?"

"You aren't trying to get to know him. You are being a pompous…"

"Piper," Griff cut me off in a gentle tone, drawing my gaze to his. "It is perfectly fine. I would be happy to answer any question your father has for me."

"You see," Dad shrugged, playing up the wide-eyed innocent look.

"I could stand to stretch my legs, Robert. Would you care to join me?" And just like that Griff and my Dad strolled from the room toward the French doors spilling onto the porch.

"I need more cake," I said to no one person in particular.

Pastor Dan slid me the whole platter, a twinkle lighting his eyes and betraying his amusement.

I did not eat the whole cake. I thought about it but only split one more slice with Sam. Unable to take the suspense any longer when Dad and Griff didn't return, I excused myself from the table and set out to find them. I would have to put a stop to the interrogation myself.

The sound of laughter floated to me as I opened the French doors of the dining hall. Light splashed onto the dark porch and illuminated an odd sight, one that had all new butterflies flitting around my stomach. Dad and Griffin sat in rocking chairs. Dad was slapping his knee, laughing at Griffin who was evidently telling a story, with enough waving of his hands for a game of charades.

I stepped onto the porch, shivering slightly as the cool breeze rolled in off of the ocean and small chill bumps jumped to attention on my arms. Dad stood when he saw me. At that moment, the French doors opened again and most of our group spilled out behind me. All except Robert and Deidra Lowe.

"Where are your parents?" I asked Sam as she stopped next to me.

"They left through the other doors. Their driver was waiting on them."

"We thought we should be getting back to the hotel. It's been a long day and I'm ready to get some sleep." Mom hugged me, "I'm sure you could use more rest also."

"I'll drive Piper home, Sam," Griff spoke as he and my dad joined us.

I cringed, waiting for Dad's objection and smart comments. None came. Kissing me on the forehead, he took Mom's hand and they followed Samantha to her yellow Juke. I smiled. I had seen my parents discreetly drop funds into the donation box, the dining hall didn't charge per plate, and was sure that Pastor Dan would be quite surprised when he got around to counting it.

Only Pastor Dan and Nora remained.

"Thank you so much for this beautiful evening," I told them. Grasping Nora's hands, I squeezed. "It was a pleasure to meet you, Nora. Pastor Dan," I turned to shake his hand, "please give my compliments to the chef. That was one of the most delicious meals I've had in weeks."

"I will do that. You two have a nice evening. I think Nora and I are going to lock up and then there is a cup of cocoa calling my name at home."

Griff hugged Dan and Nora, too. I ambled towards his silver truck, drinking in the cool night air. My eyes drank in the reflection of the moon on the ocean, my ears sighed at the lulling sound of waves pounding a slow rhythm. I leaned against the side of the cab, just gazing at the landscape.

All of the magnificence came rushing over me at once and I was so grateful that it was still a source of healing and calming feelings. On the beach last night with Abigail, I was afraid the ocean would lose its magic, that I might associate it with danger or fear but there were none of those feelings. Those were only for Abigail and, with her gone, they were quickly disappearing. I said a quick prayer of thanks for my protection and for the spectacular reminder the ocean gave of the power of my Creator.

Griff had caught up with me and now leaned past to open the truck door. I took the hand he offered to help me in, settling my small fingers in his warm palm, and hiked my dress up to make the big step up into the cab. Griff stood for an extra second and I thought he would say something but he closed the door and walked around to the driver's side. I smoothed down my dress and buckled my seatbelt.

TWENTY-ONE

We drove in silence for a time. I cranked the heater on to banish the remaining chill bumps and Griff laughed.

"Sorry, I guess I should have bought you a jacket or something to go with that," he said.

I shook my head, "No. It's perfect."

"I'm also sorry about my parents. I can't understand why they insist on being rude to you."

"Griff, stop apologizing. You didn't do anything wrong. You have been apologizing since I was in the hospital and there is no reason. You didn't hurt me. You didn't know Abigail was a nutcase. You can't control the weather or your parents. You have been kind to me. You helped find me. You made sure I had rest. You bought me this amazing gift. You've been a great friend. You are pretty incredible if you think about it." *Great, good job, excellent way to ramble Piper,* I thought, nearly face-palming myself right then; I felt so stupid.

Griff glanced over at me, then back at the road but I saw his smirk return, "You're right. I'm awesome. It took you long enough to notice though."

"Ha-ha, very funny," I joked, slapping him on the shoulder.

Griff put on the blinker and turned left into the parking lot for my apartment complex. We sat in silence a few moments after he parked.

"Let me walk you to the door," Griff spoke first.

"Okay, thanks." I slid from the truck and was making my way barefoot across the gravel, having removed my heels the moment we drove away from dinner. I cringed. I hated the feel of the rocks and grit on my feet; still, there was no way I was putting those painful shoes back on. Disgusting feet were the lesser of the two evils at this point.

All of a sudden, the rocks digging into my skin were no more, the earth disappeared from beneath my feet as Griff scooped me up and carried me straight to my apartment. My arms flew to his neck as I tried to orient myself to this new sensation. He bent and slowly placed me on my feet on the welcome mat that read "Got Chocolate?" in a curly font.

My clutch was minuscule yet, for some reason, finding my keys inside of it was a task I was utterly failing at. Swallowing my heart back down from my throat, I unlocked the door.

"Would you like to come in?" I asked.

"I would. There's something I've been wanting to talk to you about."

I gulped. "Oh. Okay."

I flipped on the lights and placed my clutch on the side table in the hall. "Make yourself at home," I pointed to the living room door. "I'll be right back after I go change."

I made my way down the short hall to my bedroom, closing the door behind me. My inner monologue couldn't decide what to wear and my headache was starting to come back. *So tired, just grab pajamas. No. No this is not a sleepover, no pajamas. Hurry, find something cute. Seriously? What is your problem Piper; just put on some clothes and get out there so Griff can tell you how embarrassed he is that Abigail thought you liked him and he can go home and you can go to bed. And stay there. Possibly forever.*

I stepped out of my gorgeous silver dress, placing it on the bed to hang up later. I settled on soft tan yoga pants and a pale purple t-shirt, the soft kind that are perfect for sleeping. Finding some fuzzy socks, my feet were probably dirty from the parking lot but oh well, I sidled into the kitchen to snag two water bottles before joining Griff in the living room.

Griff was pacing. Great, whatever it was must be really bad. I handed him a water and sat down in my cozy armchair.

"Look," I decided to beat him to the punch, "I know everything Abigail said and did probably caused a big stir with your parents. I'm very sorry. They already think I'm ruining Sam's life and now they probably see me as a greedy fortune-hunter coming after you next. I don't know how to fix it and I'm very sorry but don't worry, I'll be sure to let everyone know we are just friends. Or really, that you just came to find me because I'm your sister's friend. I'll figure something out."

Griff stood staring at me like I had lost my mind. After several awkward seconds, he recovered himself and sat down on the couch, leaning towards me. "Piper. That isn't what I was going to say at all."

"It isn't?" I squeaked.

"No."

"So, you didn't want to talk about the mess Abigail started." I had made the terrible decision to look at several Facebook posts on the way home. One of them was our very own Missy with the local news reporting the death of a "fine and upstanding citizen in her prime." Other less scrupulous media personnel were spinning a "Cat Fight Over Bachelor Golden Boy Results in Tragic Death" story on several of the more salacious sites. Evidently "Kidnapper is Killed" wasn't as good for clicks and ratings. I assumed, wrongly I guess, that Griff was getting flak from his parents and wanted to discuss what to do about them.

"Well I do but none of that was what I wanted to say."

"Okay, I'm listening."

Griffin took a deep breath and said, "First of all, I couldn't care less about all of the rumors and gossip. None of that matters. What I wanted to tell you is that I thought I felt protective of you, my sister's best friend, a younger sister type of thing. I told myself that was why I felt this desperate push to find you." He shook his head, running a hand through his dark hair absently. "The truth is, that isn't how I feel at all and the longer you were missing the less I could deny it. I don't think of you as my sister's friend. I don't even think of you as just my friend. Piper, my feelings for you go much deeper than that and I think I've known it for a while now. I didn't want to admit it. I doubt you feel the same way and I don't want to make things awkward between you and Samantha because you are so good for her."

I gaped. Like a fish. Mouth open, close, open, close. I had no words, heck at this point thoughts were proving difficult.

Griff didn't wait for a response anyway. "Piper, you're amazing. You are confident, capable, beautiful, kind, just mean enough to keep me on my toes, stubborn in the most adorable way. It wrecked me when you went missing. It nearly killed me that you were in danger because of me. And most of all, I was scared to death I would miss out on any chance of telling you how I feel."

"Listen," he knelt down in front of me and reached for my hand. "I know it is a lot to take in. I probably shouldn't have sprung it on you right now but I wanted you to know. Needed you to know."

I know, I know. By now you would think I could formulate intelligent sentences or even a bumbling bit of conversation. Instead, I heard myself say "Griff…wow…"

Knock, knock, knock.

Three sharp raps sounded at the door, causing us both to jump.

Griff dropped my hand. The moment was broken.

"That's, uh, probably Sam," I said. Griff followed me to the door, whether out of protective notions or to clobber his sister for interrupting I couldn't guess. Both thoughts made me want to giggle in a completely giddy, absolutely unacceptable way right now.

Regardless, I didn't check the peephole because I felt perfectly safe with him there behind me.

Swinging the door wide, I experience my second round of speechlessness in less than fifteen minutes.

"Piper?" the tanned, muscled guy on my doorstep asked.

"Hi?" my brain was running on less than optimum speed at this point in the evening. I tried to place this sandy-haired stranger and come up with a plausible reason for him to be at my door at this time of evening.

"Piper, it's me, It's Landon."

Keep reading for a sneak preview of book 2 in the Ooey Gooey Bakery Mystery Series as well as additional information on human trafficking.

Truly a Problem: True Information About Human Trafficking

What is it?

While this novel might be fiction, the sickening and dangerous practice of human trafficking is real, a fact of life faced by people of all ages, genders, and races. That's correct. Human trafficking victims can be male, female, young, old, native to the U.S. or a citizen of a third-world country. Below is information I gleaned from the Department of Homeland Security website and their resources. You may review the information and research courtesy of DHS at this website: www.dhs.gov/blue-campaign/tools

Human trafficking is essentially enslavement of fellow humans. As long as there is a demand for free or cheap labor, laborers who can't demand safer working conditions, or commercial sex there will be human trafficking. It is the rule of economics.

Traffickers use force, intimidation, threats, or lying to coerce men, women, and children into providing some type of labor or commercial sex. Traffickers prefer to exploit victims who are easily manipulated due to psychological or emotional vulnerability, dire economic circumstances (think homeless, foster runaway, orphaned, addictions and all those entail, unable to support a family), lacking a social safety net and more.

A number of reasons often prevent victims of human trafficking from receiving help or even from asking for help. Language barriers are one of the obvious reasons for not asking for help. Often, the victims fear physical retribution from the traffickers should they try to escape or talk to people about their situation. And, sadly, some victims fear being labeled as perpetrators by law enforcement. An example would be the crime of prostitution. That is a punishable offense and many of the participants are there willingly and deserving of arrest. Unfortunately, there are numerous people who themselves are actually victims of sex trafficking, unable to break free or scared to ask for help. When caught, rather than being provided victim services and a safe exit from that life, they are prosecuted.

Law enforcement is making great strides in trying to identify prostitutes who have been victims of human trafficking and forced into commercial sex so that a victim-centered approach can be taken. There are many resources becoming available to law enforcement that haven't always been in place and human trafficking-specific training materials are being implemented.

How to identify a victim?

The DHS website also includes a helpful list of the signs of human trafficking. As we have discussed, it is often hard to identify victims but more so when we are in denial that human trafficking occurs everywhere, including where you live most likely. Several of those signs include:

- Disconnected from any family, friends, or organizations.
- Doesn't appear at school any longer.
- Sudden or dramatic change in behavior.
- A juvenile engaged in trading sex for money or drugs or other payment.
- Persons disoriented, confused or showing signs of mental or physical abuse.
- Bruises? Breaks? Injuries in various stages of healing?
- Is the person timid or fearful?

- Does the person live in unsuitable or unsafe conditions?
- Unstable living situation and lack of personal possessions.
- A person in the control of someone else, requiring permission for where to go and who to talk to.
- Unreasonable security measures at the persons home, no freedom of movement.

NOTE: Not all of those signs are visible in every human trafficking incident, and the presence or absence of indicators does not necessarily prove human trafficking.

Who to tell?

The Department of Homeland Security would like to make it very clear that **you should not at any time attempt to confront someone suspected of human trafficking or alert the victim to your suspicions.** Doing either of these things could put you and the victim both in danger. Safety is key. You are urged instead to contact local law enforcement directly or to call the following tip lines as provided by DHS:

- Call 1-866-DHS-2-ICE (1-866-347-2423) to report suspicious criminal activity to the U.S. Immigration and Customs Enforcement (ICE) Homeland Security Investigations (HSI) Tip Line 24 hours a day, 7 days a week, every day of the year. Highly trained specialists take reports from both the public and law enforcement agencies on more than 400 laws enforced by ICE HSI, including those related to human trafficking. The Tip Line is accessible outside the United States by calling 802-872-6199. **[This information is taken directly from the DHS website.]**

- To get help from the National Human Trafficking Hotline (NHTH), call 1-888-373-7888 or text HELP or INFO to BeFree (233733). The NHTH can help connect victims with service providers in the area and provides training, technical assistance, and other resources. The NHTH is a national, toll-free hotline available to answer calls from anywhere in the country, 24 hours a day, 7 days a week, every day of the year. The NHTH is not a law enforcement or immigration authority and is operated by a nongovernmental organization funded by the Federal government. **[This information is taken directly from the DHS website.]**

If you or a local organization you are part of would like to receive Blue Campaign materials to use in raising awareness and educating the public about signs and indications of human trafficking, you can request them at no cost here:

https://www.dhs.gov/blue-campaign/request-materials

These materials may include posters, pamphlets, and cards for display and for information on how to report suspected trafficking.

Note from the Author

Thank you so much for taking the time to read Rest, Relax, Run for Your Life!

I hope that you enjoyed getting to know Piper and Sam. I also hope you were able to take the time to learn something new about human trafficking and the many lives it impacts. Unlike Piper in the book, to my knowledge I have never had a real-life encounter with this terrible practice of enslaving humans; however, it is prevalent in my county and in this country. As long as we bury our heads in the sand and allow this to be a "hidden crime" that nobody acknowledges, the perpetrators will continue to profit from this heinous way of life. This book is one tiny way I can do my part to help spread awareness.

For more about me or information on other books, visit www.katherinebrownbooks.com

Sneak Preview

Book 2 in the Ooey Gooey Bakery Mystery Series.

Knock, knock, knock.

Three sharp raps sounded at the door, causing us both to jump.

Griff and I were in my apartment. My mind reeled from the unexpected turn our conversation had taken. I expected him to deny all the rumors of a relationship between us, to insist I help convince his mother it wasn't true, and to make it clear that I was a nice girl, his sister's friend, but nothing more — imagine my surprise when instead, here he knelt on my living room floor telling me that he found me amazing, beautiful, kind, adorable (okay he might have said 'stubborn in an adorable way', I'd take it) and that he couldn't wait another moment to tell me how he felt.

Knock, knock, knock.

Griff dropped my hand. The moment shattered and vanished. I didn't have time to process these new revelations, much less form any type of response. Saved by the door.

"That's, uh, probably Sam," I said as I got up. Griff followed me to the door, whether out of some new desire to protect me or simply to clobber his sister, my best friend, for interrupting I couldn't guess. Both thoughts made me want to giggle in a completely giddy, absolutely unacceptable way that made no sense right now.

This time, I didn't check the peephole before opening the door. Despite my recent trauma, being kidnapped and nearly killed, I felt secure and safe with Griff there behind me. I never saw myself in need of a white knight but having someone there with me felt good. Swinging the door wide, I experienced my second round of speechlessness in less than fifteen minutes.

"Piper?" the tanned, trim, muscular guy on my doorstep asked.

"Hi?" it came out as a question, my brain running on less than its optimum speed at this point in the evening. I tried to place this sandy-haired stranger and come up with a plausible reason for him to be at my door at this time of the evening. I drew a blank.

"Piper, it's me. It's Landon."

I clutched at my heart in shock as recognition dawned. Too stunned to resist, I just held on as Landon scooped me up in a huge hug and spun me around the doorstep.

"Piper, are you okay? I saw the news."

"What? How are you here? What news?"

"I planned to surprise you. On the trip here to see you, I heard on the radio you were missing. Then the media said you had been kidnapped? The news showed no other headlines. They said someone was killed."

"A trip to see me? How did you know where I lived? How did you find me?"

The words rushed like a raging waterfall as we pinged questions back and forth at each other.

"Piper," another voice crashed into the moment.

I turned and exclaimed, "Griff! Griff, I'm sorry, this is my friend from school. Landon, this is Griff. He's..." I trailed off in embarrassment, dreadfully aware our important discussion had been interrupted.

"I was just leaving," Griff said. "And Landon, Piper really needs her rest as you can imagine. Do you need me to give you a ride to a hotel?"

I would have been offended at this alpha male gesture if I wasn't tickled pink on the inside and trying not to laugh on the outside. Griff crossed his arms and spread his feet wide in front of my door; it was glaringly obvious he had no intentions of leaving me alone with another man at this time of night. I yawned. Plus, he was right. This day had been too much for me. Anything else could wait until tomorrow.

"Thank you but no, I have my car. You're right. I just had to make sure Piper was okay though..." Landon turned back to me, "Piper, would you be alright with me coming to see you tomorrow, maybe taking you to lunch so we can catch up?"

"That would be wonderful," I told him. "Swing by the Ooey-Gooey Goodness Bakery anytime. I'm always there."

As Landon gave me another big hug, Griff glanced between us before dropping his eyes. "See you, Piper," he said, a slight frown tugging at his mouth, looking tired again as he turned and trudged to his truck.

I watched them both pull away, my heart aching for the conversation I botched with Griff and filled at the same time with the joy of knowing my old friend Landon was safe.

"Goodnight," I whispered to the quiet night.

Closing and locking my apartment door, I leaned back against it and sighed.

Apparently, tomorrow was going to be another long day.

~

Sleep did not come without a fight, still I did at last wrestle the pillows and my thoughts into submission. Somehow, the next morning, my eyes sprung open well before my alarm went off. I stared into the darkness toward the ceiling as I thought about the events of the last few days.

So much had happened. From winning the fundraiser contest to staying at the spa, the most luxurious place I had ever seen, to being stalked and sabotaged while there. Of course, it would be a very long time before being kidnapped by a lovesick lunatic ever left my mind. I shuddered, remembering Abigail's body splayed out on the hospital floor. Such a tragic waste of a life, all because she determined to have her fantasy marriage and lifestyle come true by any means necessary.

Then there was Griff. And Landon.

Sigh.

I threw back the covers and headed to the kitchen. Going back to sleep with so many thoughts playing tag in my head was clearly not an option. So, I did what I always do. Lose myself in my baking.

Now, I might have awoken before the alarm but that didn't mean I had a lot of time. I still needed to leave for work in about half an hour. That meant I cheated a little. Yes, I snagged the can of pre-made crescent dough from the fridge. Don't judge me.

I slathered butter in the little triangles, rolled them up, and added more butter on top. After they had baked six or eight of the ten minutes, I would add a little more butter to help them brown. Who doesn't love butter?

For the really good part though, I found the bag of butterscotch chips. My mouth watered with anticipation as I melted the butterscotch chips, brown sugar, and water together in the microwave. The delicious aroma assaulted my senses making me feel warm and cozy.

When the crescents were finished, I arranged them on a plate and poured the beautiful glaze over the tops. Crushing up a handful of walnuts, I sprinkled them over the glaze to add a little crunch.

Mmmm.

The warm glaze had me licking my lips and the crescents, now bursting with flavor, melted in my mouth. Glancing at the clock, I put a few crescents in a to-go container to take to Sam and hurried to my bedroom to get dressed.

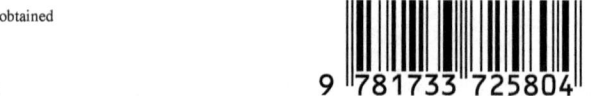